THE KEEPER OF MY KIN

The Constant Companion Tales

SALINA CHRISTMAS

The Keeper of My Kin
Copyright © Salina Christmas, 2023

A fiction inspired by legends, myths and some true events.

All rights reserved. No part of this work covered by the copyright therein may be reproduced or used in any form or by any means – graphic, electronic, or mechanical, including photocopying, recording, taping, web distribution or information storage and retrieval systems – without prior permission of the author.

ISBN: 978-1-7395631-0-3

ST⊕RY BOOKS

Published in London, United Kingdom
By Story Of Books
An imprint of GLUE Studio
www.alohaglue.com
www.storyofbooks.co.uk
Instagram: story0fbooks

Cover design: Zarina Holmes
Editor: Zarina Holmes
Typeset: GLUE Studio

DEDICATION

To my father, the soldier, who taught me that the grandest
act of heroism is forgiveness.
To my grandfather Raden Sarbini for the wonderful tales.
And to my niece Engku Anis. Keep writing.

CONTENTS

ACKNOWLEDGEMENTS

This book wouldn't be possible without the support of my family and friends. Norman and Doreen Oxlade told me some admirable stories of grit, optimism and courage of post-war London. Noriko Furukawa shared with me a most determined vision of a future anchored in peace, trust and friendship via cultural diplomacy. Nik Pollinger convinced me that one's family history must be honoured and told to the world. The advice by Paul O'Kane and Bada Song about writing filled me with optimism about the path I'm pursuing. Dr Nancy Kathleen Nanney gave me the encouragement to embrace Literature. I'm also indebted to the veterans, their children and their grandchildren whom I came across on various occasions on Remembrance Day who were generous enough to share with me a small part of their history through our conversation. Thank you for allowing me that insight into your past. Lastly, I give my thanks to the soldiers of my father's regiments, male and female, who were open enough to share their feelings and hope for humanity in front of me, a mere child at that time. You are truly my heroes.

THE
RED-HAIRED
GURKHAS

THE KEEPER OF MY KIN

The map of Camp Quetta

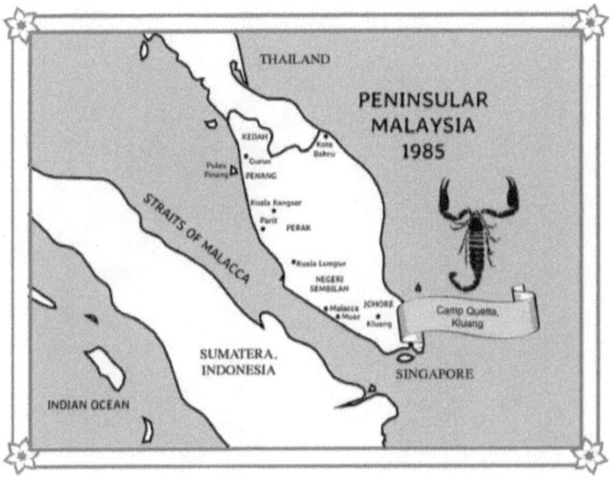

THE MAP OF CAMP QUETTA

The constant companion

An oath made in blood can't be easily undone.

When we were in primary school, our religious teacher told us that each of us are born into this world with a constant companion. A spirit. A doppelganger if you'd like. A demon maybe. My father thought it was hogwash. "A demon for each of us is too much," he said. "And there are four of you."

There were four of us: my brother Adam, me, and my younger sisters Hagar and Maryam. Then there were three of us. My brother died 15 years ago. It wasn't until his death that I gave this constant companion a thought. I agree with my father: I don't think there is one for each of us.

I think there is one for my family. He's been around for a long time.

Our father was a military officer. Wherever his regiment moved, he took his family with him. My brother, his eldest, was born during the tumultuous year of 1969. It was the year when race riots and Communist insurgency threatened to break apart Malaysia. He was a sick baby. I was born three years after him, and my sisters in the following two years. My brother grew up to be a sick boy, but one who was protective of his sisters.

In January 1981, my father's regiment relocated from Sabah, Borneo to Kluang, in the south of the Malay Peninsula. Three hours' drive from Singapore. My mother was relieved because it meant his regiment wasn't stationed at the outskirt of a jungle. At the new base, my father had more time to do sports such as tennis, sepak takraw and baseball. Our time was filled with many activities: tambola nights, barbeques, picnics, hiking, as well as watching shooting and exhibition drill competitions.

The Kluang military camp was located at the foot of a mountain. Our school was right next to the mountain, facing a secondary rainforest. From the window of our primary school, we could see black-faced gibbons swinging from tree to tree, oblivious to the humans who had encroached into their territory.

Our family accommodation, a huge four-bedroom bungalow, had a living room that faced the mountain. The room and the patio outside were separated by a set of wooden folding sliding doors. The patio faced a vast field at the back of our house, which went on for a good two to three kilometres until it met the foot of the mountain where our primary school was located.

As part of his duty as an officer, my father had to conduct spot-checks at the barracks. This happened once every few weeks. He'd bundle the four of us into his blue Peugeot and drive around. We sat restlessly in the car whilst he inspected the barracks of the privates and the adjacent bathrooms. As a child, I wondered why we had to tag along. After all, it was his job. It was later that I realised he didn't want to inspect the barracks alone. Not when most of the soldiers were out for the weekend.

The Gurkha graveyard

As a nine-year-old, I struggled to settle at the new school in Kluang. I had to leave my friends behind yet again. I missed my Sabahan schoolmates. I missed the lantern festivals. I missed the harvest festivals. I missed listening to songs in Kadazan. I missed watching Bajau warriors racing horses on the beach. I missed seeing the skulls hanging from the roof of a longhouse. Peninsular Malaysia was less fluid in cultural identity. More segregated.

Nine months into our stay at the camp, my father was given an assignment by the Commanding Officer. It was a request from the Commonwealth War Graves Commission. They had asked the Royal Malay Regiment to help with the relocation of the remains of Commonwealth soldiers that had died during World War 2.

There was a graveyard. It contained the graves of a group of fallen Gurkha soldiers. The cemetery sat at the rear end of the military base, next to a small village at the foot of the mountain. We had been to the cemetery. A few months before he received this assignment, my father, in his capacity as Quartermaster, had to oversee the distribution of clean water to the villagers when the water supply in the area was disrupted. It was the drought season. As usual, he brought the four of us along. He drove up a long, snaky and uneven clay road until we reached the back edge of the village. There, a military truck carrying water was parked by the roadside, surrounded by villagers with buckets and repurposed jerry cans. He told us to get out of the car and wait for him at the Gurkha cemetery nearby. Whilst he dealt with his colleagues and the villagers, we played hide and seek in the cemetery. It was broad daylight. We weren't scared.

"What happened to the Japanese soldiers?" I asked as we snooped around the graves.

"Don't know," my brother replied. "I don't know what they did to dead Japanese soldiers." He was a teenager. Still sickly but as sulky as the others.

He stopped to survey. "These were Gurkhas," he pronounced.

I traced my finger on some faded letters engraved on one of the tombstones. "What does it say?" I asked. My forefinger moved up and down, tracing the letters, made indistinct by time and weather.

"It's a name or something written in English," my brother said. "It's faded now."

The request from the Commonwealth War Graves Commission coincided with the arrival of a group of soldiers from New Zealand sent by their government for training. Two weeks after they arrived, the exhumation of the Gurkha remains commenced.

Because of the exhumation, my father came back from work later than usual for the next few weeks. Whilst the Kiwi soldiers were stationed at the camp, we waited in front of our house for them to pass by in their Land Rover. When they drove past, we waved and cheered: "Hello, John!". They smiled and waved back. Sometimes they stopped and gave us chocolate. We liked having them around.

My father returned home on one humid afternoon, sweaty and exhausted. This was three days after the exhumation had begun. He removed his peaked cap as he entered the kitchen where we were having tea. He had returned from the site of exhumation.

"We're looking at eight remains," he told my mother. As a Quartermaster, he oversaw the supply and logistics of everything that a regiment requires: food, drinks, ammunition, rations, housing, furniture, uniforms – anything that a soldier needed in his day-to-day job. What was not widely known was that my father also saw the logistics for funerals, the retrieval of bodies – be them soldiers or communist insurgents – and of course, the exhumation of World War 2 soldiers. My father had seen quite a few dead bodies over the years.

"They have red hair," he told my mother. "*Flaming red hair*," he emphasised.

"Father," I asked, "Don't Gurkhas have black hair?"

My father looked at me squarely in the face. "No, daughter," he said. "These ones don't."

That weekend, my father came home from his tennis session with an outrageous story shared by his tennis partner, a young lieutenant who frequently went out partying with the privates in his squad. The men told him about a so-called ghost that had been haunting the barracks and the marching field. There had been talks – and gags – about ghosts of Japanese soldiers doing formations, parade-ground drills and whatnot on that field at midnight. Usually, these were dismissed as tales to scare the wits out of those on sentry duty. However, the latest account had an uncomfortable twist to it: the men didn't think the private who suffered through one ghostly episode lied about it.

The headless captain

The private's account went like this: he had a bad fever two days before his squad were to perform an exhibition drill on the marching field. He was excused from the drill. On the day of the event – a Wednesday – he was left alone to convalesce at the barrack.

Soaked in feverish sweat, he was trembling in bed when he heard footsteps by his bedside. He opened his eyes. Through the malarial haze, he made out the silhouette of an officer. An officer of the rank of captain. He thought so because of the golden buttons on each of the epaulettes on the officer's shoulders. The uniform was green, but not the kind of deep, dark green that was of the Royal Malay Regiment. It was much lighter in shade. Years later, after my sister and I came to live in London, we came to recognise it as cypress green. This type of green isn't found within the rainforest of Malaysia. It's European green. The private was certain he wouldn't be in any trouble. He was already given leave to remain at the barrack. But there was a problem. As he glanced up further to address the officer, he saw that the chap was headless.

"Nooo!!!" my mother roared with laughter upon hearing this. "That's absurd."

"The man said it was a British army officer," my father said. He didn't laugh.

"How did he know?"

"The lieutenant's men told him that the ghost didn't want to leave the private alone. He stood there, like, forever at his bedside. The poor bastard finally noticed the three buttons on the epaulette. That ghost was a captain. So he sat up and saluted the ghost. Like he would to an officer. And the headless chap turned around and walked away."

"Where did it go?"

"It headed to the area where the bathrooms are."

My siblings and I looked at each other. We remembered the day my father returned to our car swearing profanities after he did a round of spot checks on the bathrooms. He told us he heard someone having a shower in one of the bathrooms. He looked around but there was no one.

He called out: "Anybody there?".

He went to inspect the toilet cubicles. All doors were opened except one. He knocked on that door.

"Is anybody there?" He asked. No answer. My father kicked the door open and found a young soldier having a shit. The poor soldier had a fright but managed to salute my father.

"Sorry, Sir, I am having a shit."

"Why the fuck didn't you say anything?!"

"Sorry, Sir, I'm just… I'm just having a shit."

Our father left swearing his head off. He told us this as he drove us home. We thought it was funny. He thought otherwise. Thinking back about that incident, and after hearing our father's retelling of the private's unfortunate brush with the headless soldier, we understood why our father didn't like to do his weekend spot checks at the barracks alone. He wasn't easily scared. He had spent time in battle. But he didn't know what to make of this otherworldly phenomenon. He didn't want to experience the unexplained alone.

The return of the companion

A couple of nights after the headless ghost incident, the barracks suffered a blackout. My father's batman, a young private from Kelantan – a state bordering Thailand – told my mother about a strange occurrence at the women's barrack that very night. Moments before the blackout, two female privates on the way back from the bathroom saw the headless soldier standing in the hallway, blocking their exit. It wasn't even late at night. The women screamed in horror but pushed past the apparition anyway to alert the others. Such was the discipline and courage of the female soldiers. Then the lights went out. The female soldiers at the barrack rushed outside in varying states of undress.

"Oh?" Our mother became curious. "Did my husband know about this?". The state of undress, she meant.

"Oh yes," replied the batman, oblivious to her facial expression. "He went around to check immediately. The women were in a state when the boys got there. One woman just stood there in her bra and sarong. They were in shock." He thought it was funny that the female soldiers wouldn't think twice of sticking a bayonet up a Communist's arse but were terrified of a headless ghost.

It took one week for the bodies of all the Gurkhas to be exhumed. Their remains were placed in a military mortuary for inspection whilst preparation was being made for their final resting place.

Our paternal grandfather and our aunt, my father's oldest sister, came to visit that weekend. They wanted to attend the annual Quranic recitation competition organised to celebrate the upcoming New Year. The three-night event was held on the marching field where the ghostly sightings were reported. My brother and my aunt didn't go to the competition on the first night. He wanted to watch *The A-Team* on television. My aunt stayed behind to keep him company. She was in the kitchen when she heard my brother scream in the living room. She rushed in and asked what happened. My brother pointed to one of the glass windows on the wooden folding sliding doors in the living room.

"I saw a man," he spluttered.

My aunt looked out. She saw nothing but darkness.

"I saw a man looking through the window," my brother said.

"You're imagining things," she scoffed.

She told our parents about this incident when we returned. My mother banned my brother from buying horror comics and books as a result. For the next two nights, my brother followed us to the Quranic recitation competition.

It happened again the night after the competition ended. The victim, this time, wasn't our brother. My aunt had stayed with us in the sisters' bedroom. She woke up at 5 am to perform the dawn prayer. She was already on the prayer mat when she saw, out of the corner of her eyes, the bedroom window opening. It was pushed from the outside by an arm. A man's arm. She screamed. None of us woke up. We were dead to the world. My aunt ran to the bedroom next door. My brother's. She shook him.

"Wake up! Adam? Wake up! There's a man peeping outside! Wake up!" She shouted.

My brother stayed still, as if dead. My sisters and I finally woke up. I staggered towards my aunt.

"Sarah," my aunt called out to me, "Go to your parents, now! We have an intruder! He's outside the house!".

Soon after, my father, still in his night T-shirt and sarong, surveyed the courtyard in front of the house with a torchlight. My grandfather followed behind closely with a machete, ready to strike. They found no one. My aunt swore that a man had opened our bedroom window to peer inside. He was a tall man with long straight black hair running down the side of his face. He was also shirtless. Later that day, my grandfather asked my brother if he had had a good look at the man whom he had seen a few nights before. My brother recalled that the man was tall. He had long hair. But he couldn't tell if he was shirtless. He saw the man from the neck up. The windows on the sliding door panels were high. My mother suspected a pervert. My father dismissed her notion. Every man in the military camp had short hair. The soldiers also observed the curfew strictly. For this reason, he decided not to report the matter to the military police.

It was around this time that I fell ill with fever. It could be something to do with the painful boil on my left thigh that needed looking at. I wasn't the most hygienic child at the age of nine. I was always out playing in the ditch or in the trees. It was also not my first boil or scab. But this one grew big and sore rather quickly, within a week. My parents had better things to do with my grandfather and aunt, so they asked my brother Adam to take me to the military clinic that Saturday. The clinic was next door to our school. We went early so we could return home in time to watch *America's Top 10*. It was a music TV show fronted by a DJ called Casey Kasem who wore bright-coloured jumpers. I didn't want to miss it in case Michael Jackson was on.

From our house, we walked through the vast field, mindful of snakes. I limped behind my brother. I asked him about the commotion in our bedroom the night before. He said he didn't hear a thing. He wasn't aware of my aunt trying to wake him up. He was having a strange dream.

"I saw this man in my dream. Taller than the average man. Long hair by the side of his face. He was shirtless except for a necklace on his chest. Very buff. He had this pair of baggy trousers on. Sarong around his waist.

'What are we doing here?' I asked him.

'I'm watching over you,' he said.

I don't know what language he spoke. It sounded very old. But I understood him.

'You scared me the other night,' I said. 'I don't like you peering into our living room like that.'

'I'm watching over you.'

'Who sent you?' I asked.

"And then I woke up. I heard screeching. I think auntie was angry because I didn't wake up."

I didn't think much of what Adam said when we arrived at the clinic. I was terrified at the prospect of my boil being lanced. The lump was red and sore to the touch. Fortunately, the doctor treated it with antibiotic ointment, covered it with a bandage and prescribed a course of antibiotics for me. The boil didn't pop until a few days later. Before it happened, I hobbled everywhere, dragging my left leg behind me, feeling unwell and annoyed with myself.

The haunting

We came back just in time for *America's Top 10*. Toto came on with a music video of the band members singing in between bookshelves. It was a lovely song called *Africa*. I presented my newly dressed boil to Hagar, Maryam and our mother.

Halfway through the show, we heard our father's car outside. Minutes later, he came in, wearing a white tennis T-shirt and white pair of shorts, holding a racquet.

"How was tennis?" Mother asked.

"Good. But I have something to tell you," he replied. He put down the racket on the big dining table and poured himself a cup of tea. Father sat down on the sofa next to Mother and told her the most bizarre story.

"You know Lieutenant Hassan, my tennis buddy? He said that he got chased by an unknown entity when he was out running two days ago. *I know*. It wasn't late, he said. About 5.45 pm. He did a loop from the officers' accommodation, ran past the barracks of the privates, past the marching field to the foot of the mountain, where that village is.

"It was after the Gurkha graveyard, on the way back to the marching field, that he heard someone following behind. No, hear me out. You know the snaky, gravel path that joined the village to the marching field? That one.

"Hassan said he heard running steps. At first, he ignored it but it got louder. And louder. It sounded like heavy boots on the ground, not running shoes.

Then he thought he saw, from the corner of his eyes, a figure in green running alongside him. Light green uniform. This went on for a few minutes.

"First, he was fearful. Then he got angry. So he stopped running. The 'person' beside him stopped as well. That freaked him out, so he jogged a few metres ahead. It followed. Hassan resumed his run and it went on like this until he couldn't take it anymore. So he turned around and screamed: 'Get away from me! Go! There is no god but God!'

"There stood before him the headless soldier. Three buttons on each epaulette. A captain by rank.

"Hassan trembled. He shouted: 'There is no god but God. Away!'. He muttered some holy verses, more for his courage, really. The headless soldier just stood motionless. Hassan backed away, reciting the holy verses. The ghost didn't follow. It just stood there.

"Hassan streaked to the marching field, not looking back. There, he was met by soldiers who had just finished their sepak takraw match. He told them what happened.

"It was crazy. He told me this after our tennis match. Hassan wasn't sure what it was. But he's now convinced his squaddies weren't lying about these strange happenings."

My mother took a moment to digest the story. "Maybe the men need a break. It has been a stressful time, moving from state to state," she reckoned. Within the past five years, the regiment had been relocated to three different states. The toll on well-being was immense. My mother asked our father about the Gurkha remains, exhumed almost two weeks before.

"We handed over the remains to the forensic team," he said. "The Commonwealth War Graves Commission has sent a team of experts from London to examine them. They're looking at records now to find out the regiments that were stationed here at the time of the war."

As for the ghostly fiend, our father said they were going to arrange for an officer from the religious affairs division to investigate the matter. Someone from the Military Police had also been assigned to investigate this matter – just in case it was all a hoax.

Forever my constant

A thanksgiving event comprising a prayer and a feast was organised soon after by the religious affairs department. It was tempting to think this was to do with the recent ghostly sightings. In fact, it was planned months before to celebrate our New Year which began with the month of Muharram. The Gregorian equivalent of this New Year's Day was Thursday, 29 October 1981. Muharram means "forbidden". The month of Muharram is named so because it is a period when no war is permitted. This – rather than some ghostly fiends – was of more profound significance to the soldiers. And of course, the military clerics didn't like stories of ghosts. They just about tolerated stories of jinns. In 1981, superstition was fast losing its influence on our people.

It was on that Thursday night that my fever returned. I had the creepiest dream. I was in semi-darkness, the cold damp mist clinging to my clothes. Standing before me was a European man. It wasn't the man from Toto because this man was thin, clean shaven with short hair. *Short red hair.* In the mist of the dreaming, I saw that he had a light green uniform on. His trousers were tucked into stockings and boots. There were three buttons on each epaulette on his shoulders.

"I didn't mean to scare him," he said. "I asked questions but the soldier ran away."

"I can't help you," I said, to my surprise, in a man's voice. In a language I found alien and old.

"I'd like to send a message."

"Your time in this world has passed."

"It's a very important one," he pleaded.

As he said this, seven figures emerged behind him from the darkness.

I brandished out a machete – again, to my surprise. I looked at my arm. It was sinewy, thin but powerful. It was a man's arm. On the wrist was a silver bracelet. Was this my arm, my body? I wondered. Suddenly, I found myself levitating. My body, light as a feather, drifted back in retreat. The man and the other figures grew smaller beneath me. Did I float or did I grow bigger? I couldn't tell.

"I'd like to send a message to my mother," said one of the figures. It was a very young man with pale skin. His auburn hair was partly obscured under a black beret, the band decorated with red-and-white dice pattern.

"I have a message for my children," said another, slightly older, with lighter copper hair, but also wearing the same type of headgear.

And then all of them spoke at once, each asking me to send a message to their loved ones. Their voices echoed and echoed until the dream was broken by my aunt's voice. She woke me up. She said I talked in my sleep.

The next day, my grandfather asked me about my dream. He had been informed of Adam's dream and the ghostly sightings we had heard of. He inspected my boil and felt the temperature on my forehead with his hand. After Friday prayer, and when my father returned to his office, my grandfather performed a special ritual at home. He told us to gather seven types of white flowers, which we happily did. He recited a mantra, a mixture of Javanese and holy verses. He then went to the four corners of our home to sprinkle water, salt and flowers. Witnessed by my family, he blessed me with holy water and white flowers. Basically, I was told to crouch down in my T-shirt and pants in the backyard. He poured the bucket of water over my head. He told us not to venture out to the field behind our house after dusk. He told us not to tell our father about this ritual for fear of upsetting him. That Sunday, my grandfather and my aunt returned to their village.

It wasn't until years later that I found out that my grandfather, prior to his pilgrimage to Mecca in the mid-80s, had liberated a constant companion – a guardian of the family, if you'd like – to comply with the sacredness of religious observance. The constant companion was meant only to serve him in his younger days. In his days as a newly arrived migrant in the peninsular, the companion helped my grandfather clear farmlands. During the time of the Japanese occupation, the companion went a bit further in his duty to protect our family. But that's another story.

It was alleged that we had a guardian who had been around, perhaps too long, in our family for generations. My father rejected this notion, himself very much against superstition. My sisters and I did wonder if the long-haired phantom was the constant companion. My brother is now dead, and I can't compare notes on our dreams of this 'thing'. The companion didn't appear to me for a long time. He did so to my brother a few times whilst Adam was alive. Apparently, he appeared – unasked – when he felt my grandfather's family members were in danger. After a time, this became an inconvenience. Before his death, our grandfather decided to liberate this companion.

What he neglected to tell us is that the constant companion doesn't have free will. He had to be passed on to a new master.

Two weeks had passed since the remains of the Gurkhas were exhumed and transferred to the mortuary. There were no more ghostly sightings. Some of the soldiers thought the thanksgiving event had been a success in getting rid of them. We'd never know for sure. My father completed the mission given to him. He approved for the remains to be transferred to a proper Commonwealth war grave. He was pleased to see them off. After two weeks, my father finally had a quiet Saturday. He was happy not to have spent another weekend looking at old corpses.

"Are they going to be given a Hindu burial?" My brother asked him whilst all of us were lounging around in the living room watching *Bintang RTM* or RTM Stars, a talentime show on Malaysian national television.

"Who?"

"The Gurkhas."

"Oh. They weren't Gurkhas," my father said. We peeled our eyes away from the television to look at him. "They're not?" I asked.

"No. We had pathologists and forensic anthropologists to examine the remains. The red hair. We think they belonged to one of the Scottish regiments."

My father explained that the Commonwealth commission did a research on the area and found no evidence of Gurkhas being stationed there during the war.

The 2nd Argyll and Sutherland Highlanders had arrived in Malaya in the late 1930s as part of the 12th Indian Infantry Brigade. In 1941, together with the Plymouth Argyll Royal Marines and the 11th Indian Division, they were left to hold back the Japanese incursions in the north whilst other regiments fled by sea and air. The Slim River land siege in the state of Perak in January 1942 was particularly brutal. Out of thousands, less than one hundred Argylls returned to the frontline. The rest fled to the jungle or to neighbouring Indonesia, or were captured, or killed.

Kluang, being a halfway point between Kuala Lumpur and Singapore, was a vital town for the Japanese to seize. The men left defending our military camp, Camp Quetta, were most likely the Argylls. In 1981, when DNA technology was at its infancy, the forensic anthropologists had only bones to go by. But they confirmed the red-haired Gurkhas weren't Gurkhas. It was likely that the Argylls were left to defend our military camp whilst the British and the Anzacs retreated to Singapore. Many were slain by the Japanese. The eight men were lucky to have been buried at all. But there was a sad story behind the burial. It was common for Japanese soldiers to order their prisoners to dig their own graves before their execution. The forensic anthropologists reckoned the eight men were executed by the Japanese. One of the remains was found to have his head severed from his body. Looking at the marks of cut at the base of the skull, they deduced that he was probably beheaded with a katana. They reckoned he was the leader of the group. He was probably an officer. A captain.

We listened intently to my father. "What are they going to do with the bodies?" my brother asked.

"They will be given a Christian funeral and buried in a consecrated ground in accordance with their religion," my father replied. "There was a priest amongst the group of Kiwis that came over for training recently. He performed the last rite for them before we sent the remains away. They're probably returned to where their regiment came from."

We stared at our father silently, saddened by his account.

I didn't dwell much on what happened in October 1981 until I visited Berlin, Germany, in winter 2008. My childhood was spent in the Cold War, on the democratic side, so I was curious to see the other side of the fence. I visited the Bundestag to look at the newly renovated parliament – and to inspect the bullet holes left in the walls.

Out of curiosity, I checked out what was left of the Berlin Wall. I inspected the names of soldiers who died trying to flee Eastern Germany via this wall. I recalled the 1984 hit by the German band Alphaville, *Forever Young*. It was my brother's favourite song. For a moment, I was transported to Camp Quetta, to the mountain, to the 'Gurkha' graveyard, to my brother and to that strange dream I had of the men in their cypress green uniforms. I was too young to understand what it all meant. Standing before the Berlin Wall, I tried to make sense of things. After a while, I stepped back and decided: there were no ghosts.

I gave the Unterwelten underground tour a miss, however. I wasn't about to ruin my dark, winter holiday in Berlin with the meddling of a constant companion.

THE KEEPER OF MY KIN

THE
TIGER-MAN
AND HIS
CONSTANT
COMPANION

The paternal bloodline

The Raden Family Tree

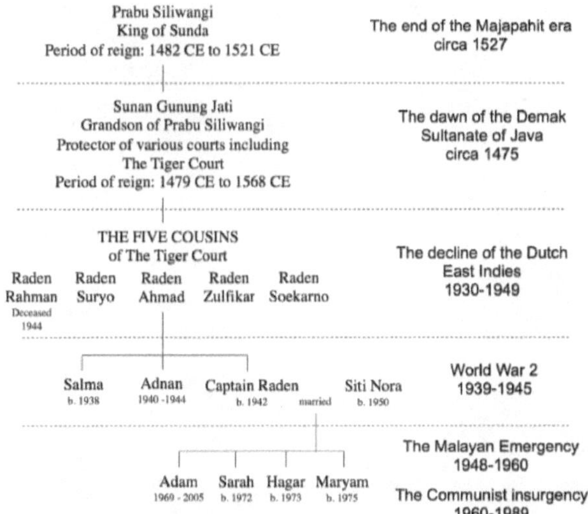

32

The keepers of my father's kin

This is the story of the keepers of my fathers' kin. They've been prescribed a life of violence which is none of their choosing. If we fight, we torture them with our demands, subjecting them to grief and unhappiness. If we don't fight, the enemies will come at us. We're fearful of the keepers' rage. But master them we must, or else our clan shall perish.

The hour of the tiger

If you seek revenge, dig two graves.
One for yourself and one for your enemy.

It wasn't clear to me of my grandfather's dark art in the supernatural until I was about to enter high school. It was 1984. I'd just turned 13. We were three years into our stay at the military base in Kluang, in the south of the Peninsular Malaysia. My brother Adam, 16 years of age, got shipped to a boarding school, to his dismay. My younger sisters Hagar and Maryam were still in primary school.

The Hat Yai Treaty was five years away. The Communist insurgency showed no sign of de-escalating. My father's regiment was about to be re-deployed to the dense jungle of Grik, a town bordering Malaysia and Thailand. His captaincy was increasingly becoming a source of stress to him and our mother. The Communists had, by this time, progressed from sniping and Molotov cocktail ambushes to dismemberment using landmines.

In retaliation, our country's regiments hounded them deep into the jungle. The Thai regiments blocked them on the other side of the border. The belligerent got increasingly desperate and violent. They directed their ire towards the East-West Highway construction that stretched from the East Coast to the West Coast of the peninsula.

In late 1982, just over a year after we moved to Kluang, my father's regiment was sent off to Grik for three months. A few months before, a group of construction workers working on a section of the highway were ambushed and killed by the Communists. The engineer supervising the site was kidnapped. He was later found dead, shot in the head. A battalion comprising the Royal Malay Regiments and the Royal Ranger Regiment – our equivalent of the British SAS despite its unassuming name – was deployed to protect the highway construction. The operation was known as Operation Barrier. Scores of soldiers died, some in battle, some due to the land mines. Several were from my father's regiment.

The paradox began at this juncture. My sleep-talking ceased after my grandfather performed a ritual in October 1981. There were no more sightings of the headless soldier that, for over two weeks, scared the soldiers senseless in the Kluang military base. On the contrary, my father's sleep-talking worsened after he returned from his first mission to Grik. My grandfather dismissed it, insisting that his son got it from his grandfather and his great-grandfather. I wasn't convinced. In his sleep, my father recited the last rite. He cried: "There is no God but God". At times, he mumbled incoherently.

My father, as a Quartermaster, was in charge not only of the logistics of men, food and ammunition. He had overseen the transportation of dead bodies of both our soldiers and the enemies. He and his fellow combatants had whispered the last rite into the ears of dying soldiers.

In January 1984, we were informed that in five months, his regiment was to be deployed to Grik for the third time. Eager to prolong his son's luck, my grandfather organised a massive thanksgiving event at his home in the state of Malacca, 120 km away from where we lived. It took place in the first ten days of Aidilfitri. In Gregorian terms, that was from 31 May to 9 June 1984.

My brother returned home from boarding school to join us for the thanksgiving. My father's family and his siblings' families gathered at our grandfather's. My grandfather also invited his three cousins for the event. These were cousins whom he sailed with from Cirebon, Java, to the peninsula in the 1930s, when they were teenagers.

All but one turned up.

One of my grandfather's cousins – Wak Suryo or Grandfather Suryo as he was known – suggested that we visit the absent cousin, Karno. "I heard he's under the weather lately," he said. "I'll give his son and daughter a call. We can visit him tomorrow." Karno's children were contacted. They were more than happy to receive us at their father's home. The three cousins – my grandfather Ahmad, Suryo and Zulfikar – and our family travelled by car to Karno's place in Muar, about 16 km away.

What greeted us was macabre bordering on ghoulish. Karno, his son Yusof and his daughter Habsah, welcomed us at their front porch. The lawn, overlooking the foreshore of the River Muar, was neatly cut and trimmed. There were no trees, however. His wooden timber house was like any other Malaccan house: dark brown, ornate with glass-stained windows and majestic on stilts. But there was something odd. Nailed to the wall next to the front door were a grass sickle, a rusty machete, a fishnet and – I kid you not – a spear. The sickle and machete were too utilitarian to be ornamental, but Karno was a farmer, so who knows? The fishnet reeked of eccentricity, but the spear threw us off. Our entourage looked at each other, baffled. My grandfather broke the awkward silence by conveying his greeting of peace to his cousin. Peace be with you, Karno reciprocated. He and Karno exchanged pleasantries in low Javanese.

"Kabare?" *What's the news?*

"Waras." *All is well.*

I noticed that Karno limped when he walked. He seemed to be dragging his left leg slightly. Of course, this was hardly irregular compared to what we were to witness later.

Inside, we were entertained with savoury finger foods, biscuits and tea. The cousins conversed in Malay, and then in low Javanese, and then in high Javanese when they began to reminisce on their times in Java. Our father followed silently. The rest of us could hardly understand them.

We scanned the living room in discreet horror, as politely as we could. There was a dried-up spider skewered with a pin to the wall, as big as one's palm. In one corner was a dried-up centipede, also impaled in the same disturbing manner. In another was a darkened out-of-shape ball – possibly a very old egg – spiked to the wall with the thin, sharp blade of a pair of scissors. Where Karno sat, there was a keris – a dagger – on the wall above his head. Karno's children looked very embarrassed. We, in turn, were embarrassed for them.

The elderly cousins broke their Javanese exchanges for Karno to ask my father in Malay:

"When are they sending your troops to Grik?"

"June," my father answered. "End of this month."

"What will they have you do there?"

"I'll be overseeing the supplies for the regiment. The frontline team will sweep the landmines. We will watch over the East-West highway construction."

Karno nodded. His cousins looked at his face intently. Perhaps too intently. Silence fell across the room.

I spotted a gambus – the Malay equivalent of the European lute – on a shelf, and spontaneously asked Karno:

"Do you play that, Wak?"

Karno smiled. He cast his eyes to the gambus and cheered up.

"I used to. I was in a ghazal band a long time ago."

Zulfikar interjected: "He used to play the Sundanese kecapi, too, back in the days."

"Really?" I said. I imagined Karno as a young man playing the zither and that lute.

The conversation then shifted to the last rounds of the national talentime show, *Bintang RTM*, on who we'd think would make it to the final. That saved the occasion, somehow.

We went home in silence. My grandfather was rather pensive for the rest of the holiday, only brightening up in the company of his cousins, who stayed for two more days. Out of his earshot, my father aired his concern over Karno's well-being to our mother. We were having tea with our aunt – his eldest sibling – and Zulfikar, when my father let slip that Karno had been practising witchcraft. My grandfather, Suryo and the others were away visiting a relative, so this delicate conversation could be had at last.

"It seemed to have gotten out of hand and driven him mad," our father observed.

"He's stopped practising that a long time ago," my aunt countered.

"He should have got rid of *those things* on the wall."

My brother marvelled: "Did you see the *dead spider*?"

"As big as your face," my sister Maryam exclaimed, holding her palm up, fingers spread out.

My aunt pressed on: "I had spoken to Yusof and Habsah. They wanted to clean up the house. He wouldn't let them. Not yet anyway."

Zulfikar quietly chimed in: "He wasn't always like that."

We looked at him in silence.

"He used to love his music and songs," Zulfikar said. "Karno was the liveliest of us all. We thought Malacca was where we'd find our happiness. Java was full of hardship. We were happy for a while. Then the war broke out."

Cousins from the Tiger court

1935

Zulfikar said there were five of them, initially. Lads of not even 18 who wanted to be free of the Dutch, keen to find a life outside the keraton – the royal court. The cousins were young nobility from one of the several royal courts that still survived in Cirebon. The royal standard flown was that of a tiger called Macan Ahmat.

Times were tough in the 1930s. Years of botched-up – and enforced – plantation practices by the Dutch East India Company led to intensive farming that, in turn, resulted in famine and rebellion. The Netherlands government took over. The royal court capitulated to the Dutch. The Great Depression happened. Poverty afflicted the region. The cash-strapped Dutch taxed citizens for ridiculous things such as cobwebs in buildings. Desperate times, desperate measures.

The lads acknowledged their time as royals was up. Titles were meaningless in the face of poverty. They had good innings as nobility, but it was time to let go. They boarded the ship bound for Malacca: Raden Rahman, Raden Soekarno, Raden Soerjo, Raden Zulfikar and my grandfather, Raden Ahmad. Raden Soekarno, the youngest of them, wept as the ship disembarked. My grandfather didn't. "What's the point of crying?" He objected. "We've made up our mind."

When they arrived in Malacca, the lads dropped their honorific title, "Raden", which means "prince". They were known simply by their given names: Rahman, Karno, Suryo, Zulfikar and Ahmad. They became commoners.

The cousins worked as farm hands. They cleared lands and dug canals. They settled with local women, had children and lived as respectable locals. My grandfather's diligence won the respect of his employer, a Buginese-Malay merchant who owned several farms. He married off his middle daughter – my grandmother – to my grandfather. By 1940, my grandfather had two children: my aunt Salma and a son, Adnan. Royal habits die hard, however. My grandfather didn't arrive empty-handed. He brought with him a most indispensable servant: the constant companion, the keeper of his family and kin. The ghostly inheritance passed down from generation to generation. How else did he manage to clear those massive tree trunks felled by his cousins?

He was careful to use the constant companion only for farm work. My grandfather observed the prayers, the fasting and he read the holy book regularly. He stayed away from black magic. Everything was fine until the war broke out.

The map of the Tiger-Men

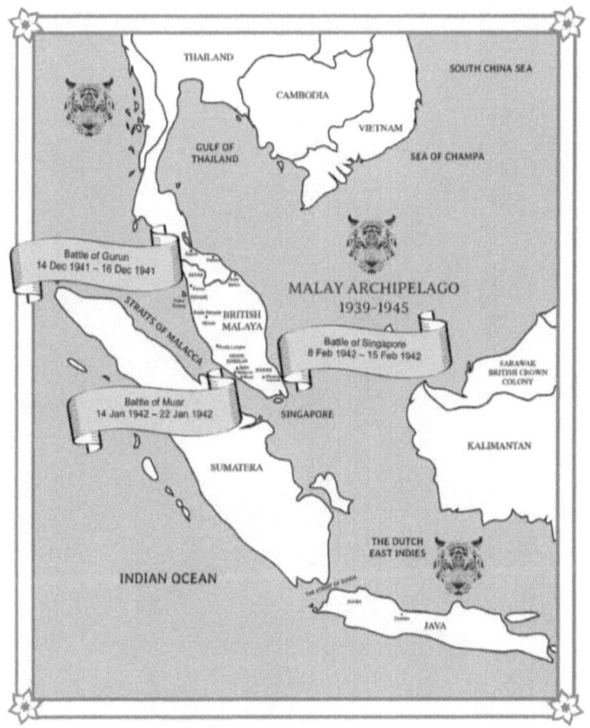

THE MAP OF THE TIGER-MEN

A star in the darkest night

1942

The Imperial Japanese Army finally raided our part of the peninsula in January 1942. They were under-prepared for jungle warfare, and that would bite them back. But the war had dragged on too long. Their motherland, pummelled from all sides, desperately needed rubber and tin. Plenty of them. The Imperial Japanese Army annihilated the 45th Indian Infantry Brigade at the north of the River Muar, barely 30 km away from our village. And that was the last big showdown of the Malayan Campaign.

News of rape and massacre reached the village. But my grandfather couldn't flee with his family. My grandmother was eight-months pregnant. He and his cousins, along with other villagers, were forced to build an airstrip. The Japanese wanted to hit Singapore next by air. Put in charge to oversee the construction was Captain Nagayama Kyomi of the 5th Imperial Guard regiment and Sergeant Yoshimura Eita. The latter was a kempeitai man. He was bad news. Fortunately, the constant companion was there to help the cousins with the hard labour, clearing tree trunks in the cover of night.

In February 1942, my grandmother went into labour. It was night time. Japanese fighter planes were flying overhead to bomb Singapore. My grandfather put out all the lights, lest they got mistaken for a target. My father was born, a star in the darkest night. My grandfather named him Raden to remind himself that princes were made for times like this.

But even princes could only take on so much.

Not long after Singapore fell, a local man named Lok was wickedly murdered for nothing. The son of the local shopkeeper, he was clearing his land by burning the tall grass and rubbish when the kempeitai rounded him up. They accused him of sending smoke signals to the anti-Japanese resistance. Lok swore this wasn't the case. Sergeant Yoshimura forced him to dig his own grave. Lok wept as he did so. He was beheaded afterwards.

The kempeitai and their fellow soldiers proceeded to rounding up other Chinese families in the village – the ones that didn't manage to flee. Babies were snatched from their mothers and thrown in the air to be impaled with bayonets. They were disembowelled before their mothers' eyes. Young girls were taken to school, raped and then shot dead. Their bodies were buried in the school field.

As soon as my grandfather made it to the list of forced labourers for the Burmese railway project, he knew they had to escape.

He bribed the procurement agent – a Malay man, traitor to his race and country – with his most prized possession, a golden belt with a diamond-studded buckle.

Growing up as a boy prince, his older sister would secure his sarong with the belt when she dressed him up. The belt reminded him of her. He gave this up in exchange for his freedom and took his family into the jungle.

Cloaking spells and death spells

1943 – 1944

My grandparents took their children through the stinking mangrove swamps, along the shoreline and then into the jungle. They avoided the River Muar, where British and Indian soldiers were massacred by the hundreds.

My grandfather built a makeshift shelter camouflaged by tree branches. In the nearby brook, they washed to keep the mosquitos away. The insects couldn't be smoked out. Burning would reveal their hiding place. My grandfather made a staff out of tas wood. He put a spell on it. He told my aunt it was to fend off wild animals "and other things".

For several weeks, things were bearable. My aunt, only five years of age, looked after her younger brothers whilst our grandparents foraged for food.

One afternoon, my grandfather hastily beckoned the family to return to their shelter. They huddled behind the curtain of branches and leaves. My grandfather silently mouthed a prayer. His grip on the staff tightened. Moments later, through the camouflage, they saw three Japanese soldiers walking into view. Rifles in hand, the soldiers walked cautiously, surveying the area. A few minutes later, they were disturbed by the sound of a broken branch. In the distance, between the trees, a figure stood waiting. Male, tall, long hair, bare-chested. The soldiers, agitated, ran towards the figure. They didn't return.

It was a miracle that the soldiers didn't notice the shelter. It was barely ten metres away, not even well-covered. It was as if the shelter was invisible. Of course, my grandfather didn't mouth any good old prayers. He casted a cloaking spell.

The following night, my grandfather woke up my aunt. He told her to keep watch over her mother and little brothers. He left with his wooden staff, and returned some two hours later, covered in blood. It wasn't his. With him was a British soldier. A thin, young man, skin reddened by the sun, his eyes big and bewildered. His red hair was matted with dirt and sweat.

In broken Malay, he told the family that he was of the Argyll and Sutherland Highlanders regiment. He escaped into the jungle after the regiment's defeat up north. He then joined a covert operation in the Malacca area. Someone betrayed his unit to the Japanese. He ran away, pursued by three Japanese soldiers. The night my grandfather saved him, the soldiers were closing in on him. Exhausted, the Argyll thought he was going to be caught. But the soldiers pursuing him disappeared one by one. He wasn't sure how. He had no time to look behind. He heard yelps. Totally spent, he collapsed to the ground. When he looked up, he saw what he thought was a rather frightening-looking man standing above him. Tall, long hair, bare-chested save for a thick necklace, holding a machete. He blinked back in confusion. *No*, it wasn't a tall man with long hair. It was my grandfather, holding a staff.

The hideout was no longer safe. The family and the Argyll retreated deeper into the wilderness. They built another camouflaged shelter. At a secret meeting point, my grandfather caught up with his contact and passed on a message. Two weeks later, two men in combat fatigues turned up, a British soldier and a local Chinese man. The Brit was formerly of the East Surrey Regiment, one of the 200-odd men who survived the assault of 1941. The other was from a local paramilitary group. His green cap had a red star. He was from the Malayan Communist Party. They picked up the Argyll and made their way to their secret HQ in the jungle of Perak, by an obscure river that flows downstream into the royal town of Kuala Kangsar.

Not long after, Adnan – my grandparent's eldest son – not yet four – succumbed to beriberi. My aunt was particularly crushed. She had missed meals so her brothers had enough to eat. But poor Adnan needed more than insects and wild roots for food. My grandmother wrapped his tiny body in a worn-out batik cloth. The family emerged temporarily from the jungle to have him buried at the nearest village, in an unmarked grave.

Dig two graves

1945

The cousins, Suryo and Zulfikar, sought out the bereaved family some two months later. My grandfather, sensing their arrival, waited patiently, the tas staff resting on his lap. They arrived with devastating news. Rahman, their eldest cousin, was executed by the Japanese along with his son. Someone ratted on them. The kempeitai found out about the radio they hid at home. They were accused of colluding with the late Lok, which wasn't true. They didn't indulge in any anti-Japanese activities. They just wanted to hear the latest news on the war. The kempeitai took them away. The women of the family offered jewellery to free them, to no avail. The son, only a boy, was beheaded in front of Rahman before he was put to the sword. Captain Nakamura gave the order, Sergeant Yoshimura carried out the execution. Then the kempeitai dumped their bodies in a mass grave, where other decomposing bodies were already piling up. They were to be burnt later. That night, the three cousins and a few villagers came to collect the remains. Choking back their tears, the men transported the bodies to a local cemetery. There was no shroud available, so the remains were wrapped in banana leaves. They were given the last rite and buried discreetly in one grave. The grave was camouflaged with leaves and tree branches.

My grandparents wept angrily as they listened to the cousins' account. Wiping away his tears, my grandfather asked: "Where's Karno?"

"He's gone missing," Suryo replied.

"Missing? How?"

"He left after the incident with no message."

"How can he just leave? It's dangerous out there."

"He's not taken, we're sure of that."

"What do you mean 'not taken'?"

"Ahmad, he took it the worst. He was beside himself. Now he's gone. We came here because we need your help. Karno must be found. *Soon.*"

My grandfather understood the implication. The cousins feared the worst.

The family abandoned their shelter to move into Zulfikar's home in Jasin. Once resettled, the three cousins searched for Karno. Around June 1945, news trickled in about a tiger on a rampage, killing chickens, goats and cows in a frequency unnatural of the tiger. A tiger kills only when it needs to feed. The recent killings, however, happened in quick succession.

Then words came with regards to the Imperial Japanese soldiers who were posted at my grandparents' village in Merlimau. Seven soldiers were found dead at their post. Captain Nagayama, Sergeant Yoshimura and four of their men were found in pieces in their barrack. Outside, a sentry was found dead, also in a similar condition. The villagers assumed they were eaten by a tiger. A tiger with an appetite big enough for seven grown men. They also found bloodied footprints all over the place. Human footprints.

The boy soldier who saw everything

September 1945

According to Zulfikar, the most damning account of the were-tiger incident came from a Japanese soldier who survived the bloodbath.

Yamashiro Ryu was only 15 when they shipped him to Malaya in March 1945. By this time, Japan had sacrificed far too many young men. The military had run out of university students intensively procured for kamikaze and other campaigns. So it turned to schoolchildren. Students of 15 and above such as Yamashiro were conscripted.

Yamashiro was a late developer, very much a child at heart. After his mother's death, the schoolboy was considered another mouth to feed to his relatives. Several months after the unfortunate passing of his mother, the headmaster of his school whom he looked up to as a father figure was taken away by the authority under the charge of lèse-majesté: the old man had spoken up against the conscription of students. He had committed treason against the Emperor.

The schoolboy Yamashiro was sent to Malaya as a conscript towards the end of World War 2. He was frightened, but grateful that his destination was Malaya, not Burma, or worse, the Nakajima aircraft squad.

The only keepsake he took to the volatile Malayan land was his late mother's prayer beads. He was withdrawn, his sullenness mistaken as aloofness by his comrades. For whatever reason, he got on the bad side of Captain Nagayama and the more senior ranks from day one. Because he was

Japanese, they stopped short of killing him. Instead, they gave him a hard time. He was excluded from group socials. Which was fine by Yamashiro because that meant he had no hand in the drinking and gang-raping that was going on.

During kendo training, he got prodded in the neck with the shinai – whilst not in body armour or head guard. At one time, after a bad session, he thought he wouldn't be able to swallow food again. The bullying began after he was sent to oversee his first burial and burning of the executed. Sickened by the sight and smell, Yamashiro vomited on the spot. For this, he was punched in the head. Since then, he was assigned two tasks: to watch over the local school and observe the two teachers and the pupils; and to perform sentry duty at the watchtower every other week during graveyard shift. Two soldiers had already been taken out by sniper's bullets at that blasted watchtower. The seniors deemed the boy fit for the next bullet. For Yamashiro, the bullet – and the mosquitoes – were preferable.

Because of the proximity of his age to the pupils', Yamashiro got on well with them. He picked up rudimentary Malay from the Malay lesson. He helped the pupils with their Japanese lesson. He befriended the Malay teacher, a man named Che Mat son of Ali. It was around the time of the tiger rampage in June that he first heard of the beast. "Siluman harimau" according to the Javanese pupils. "Harimau jadian" to the Malay ones. They meant the same thing: were-tiger. He asked the pupils if it was a deity, Yamashiro being a believer of kami-sama after all. This wasn't a deity, the pupils insisted. It was something unholy. They were convinced it wasn't just any tiger. Human footprints were found at the scene of crime. The attacks on the livestock appeared targeted, too. Yamashiro put two-and-two together. The livestock targeted belonged to the people who ratted on the Rahman family. The locals believed they were revenge attacks. The were-tiger was seen roaming outside the owners' homes at night.

When Yamashiro was given the graveyard shift at the watchtower for the whole month of August, he didn't complain. He was instructed to mind his unit's post at night during the spate of 'tiger attacks'. The mosquitoes, stray bullets and heavy rain were the least of his concern. Yamashiro could sense something ominous looming.

All over the country, Japanese soldiers were already thin on the ground. Many succumbed to starvation and diseases. Many more got killed in combat. The fatal night happened the week after the unit got the news about Hiroshima and Nagasaki. The six men were already blind drunk, deep in their sorrow but relieved at the prospect of going home.

It wasn't even midnight when the tiger emerged. It crept into the wooden barrack and silently charged at the drunken men. There was no warning because the sentry stationed outside the barrack was the first to be mauled to death by the beast. To Yamashiro, it happened so fast.

The beast swallowed a soldier's head whole and bit down to crush his skull. After casting the lifeless body aside, it grabbed the next soldier by his leg with its human-like hand, yanked him closer and sank its claws into the poor sod's belly to scoop his guts out.

With a spirited shout, Sergeant Yoshimura sank his bayonet into the back of the beast's left thigh. The creature roared. It pulled the blade out, yanked the bayonet off Yoshimura's hands and rammed it through his heart. Angered, it lunged at the dazed soldier and bit his head off. As the headless Yoshimura staggered about, the beast maimed the other two men. Captain Nakamura, in his drunken haze, stumbled for the exit. The beast caught him. It ripped off his left leg from the knee down. Then it bit off his right foot. Nakamura let out a blood-curdling scream. As he trashed about in pain, the beast returned to the two he maimed earlier. It ate their insides whilst they were still alive.

The beast saved the best for last. It toyed with Nakamura like a cat would with its live food. It swiped him to the left and to the right. It bit chunks out of his body. It sat on him for a bit. It shook him about like a rag doll. Then it snacked on him as his life ebbed away.

Yamashiro witnessed all this from the watchtower. He

could have fired a warning shot when he saw the tiger approaching the barrack. But he didn't. He was transfixed by its ghastly appearance: top half tiger, bottom half human – but with the tail of a tiger. The hands and feet were human-like, but with claws. Yamashiro also had the opportunity to shoot the beast. He had the vantage point and position. Yet he did nothing. He simply watched the beast move from one man to the next. When it got too much, he closed his eyes and chanted "Amida Buddha, Amida Buddha". Hands trembling, he fished out the juzu beads his mother left him, and held them to his chest.

The were-tiger stopped after it had its fill of the seven men. Yamashiro, his arse numb from crouching in the same position for hours, shifted uneasily. The juzu beads slipped and fell to the ground. *"Shit!"* He hissed, and immediately regretted his swearing.

The tiger's ears pricked up. It prowled towards the watchtower. It inspected the juzu beads on the ground. The beast picked up the beads and sniffed. Yamashiro intensified his chanting, wetting his pants at the same time. If his life were to end at that moment, he'd like to be reunited with his beloved mother. He'd like them to be reborn together in the next life.

The beast stayed motionless for a while. Its ears twitched as it listened to his chanting. It was as if it could understand him. Then, it lowered its head to the ground. Slowly, the beast walked away, the juzu beads dangling from its mouth. The boy soldier wasn't the enemy it was looking for.

Yamashiro waited until sunrise before he climbed down. He didn't bother to check the bodies of his colleagues. He dashed to Che Mat's home. In Japanese and pidgin Malay, he told him about the incident. He implored Che Mat to hide him away. The teacher dressed him up like a local and sent him to live with his cousin, a fisherman in neighbouring Muar.

When the Japanese later made the grisly discovery of their colleagues, they didn't bother to look for Yamashiro. He was assumed dead. When the Communists took over the area in the last two weeks of August, they, too, didn't bother to seek him out. The British moved in swiftly by September, pushing the Communists into a hasty retreat. It was their turn to make the grim discovery of the rotting mutilated remains. They also didn't bother to look for Yamashiro. When Japan surrendered and the Imperial Japanese Army was recalled home later that month, Yamashiro didn't make himself available or known. He was sent to die in Malaya, so he was as good as dead to those at home.

He remained a fisherman for a good few years before opening a bicycle shop. He settled with a Malay lady and had five children. He acquired a new name: Arshad. From the 1970s onwards, Yamashiro was known as Haji Arshad son of Abdullah, a respected elder of his village. By the time of his death in the 1990s, nobody saw him as Yamashiro Ryu. And no one mentioned the fatal night of the were-tiger.

The revelation

September 1945

The cousins' worst fear was realised. The Tiger-Man, another constant companion – a family inheritance much older and nastier – had been unleashed. And he had tasted human blood.

As soon as the cousins heard about the tiger attacks, they got word that Karno had been staying at a plantation near Gambir Hill. The message was delivered by a boy, the son of Ah Kim, the plantation supervisor. He was Lok's cousin. Suryo, Zulfikar and my grandfather went to see him. Ah Kim said he was sorry to hear about Rahman and his family. Karno came to him not long after the incident. Out of pity, Ah Kim hired him as his farm hand because of their shared losses. Karno had been very diligent – until he got rather ill recently. He started vomiting strange things.

"Like what?" My grandfather asked.

"Chicken feathers," Ah Kim replied. "Lots of chicken feathers."

Ah Kim feared it was santau – a heinous type of Malay black magic that sees victims puking anything from broken glasses to barbed wires.

"When did this happen?" Suryo probed.

"Two months ago," Ah Kim said. "He bounced back quickly, though. But last week he got ill again. I fear for his life."

"Where is he?" My grandfather asked.

"In one of the worker's huts. I'll take you there."

Ah Kim led the three cousins to Karno's hut. It was noon.

The door was shut. My grandfather, gripping his tas staff, signalled the cousins to perform their prayer. Ah Kim, creeped out, asked: "What's going on?". Zulfikar turned around and said: "If we get into trouble, *run*."

The cousins entered the hut one by one. My grandfather was ready to strike Karno – or whatever that beast was – that was lying in bed, sweating and chuffing like a cat. His upper left thigh was in a bandage, blood seeping through the cloth. The person on the bed turned to look at his visitors. His skin was grey. He'd lost a lot of blood. He looked like Karno. But the cousins weren't fooled.

"There is no God but God," the cousins invoked repeatedly. "We seek forgiveness from God."

Karno's eyes welled up. He knew how he was perceived by his cousins. Slowly, Karno sat up. He coughed, and with a sigh, leaned forward to expel phlegm, blood, bits of flesh, bones and human fingers.

"Cousin", he said, scanning the horror on the floor, "I'd like to go home."

It took a week to exorcise the beast out of Karno. It wasn't easy. In the first few days, he had to be tied down. The cousins washed him, prayed for him, looked at his injury and took turns reading the holy book to calm him down. Karno was fine most of the time, but there were moments when he, or that thing, trashed about in discomfort. When he did so, the cousins reminded him that he had to let go of his constant companion.

"Why should I? He protected me," Karno protested, but at the same time looking like he was very much at death's door. The witchcraft was consuming his life slowly.

"What you did was evil. You're associating God with the devil," Suryo countered.

"I only summoned what's within me. It's my birthright, and it's *your* birthright," Karno insisted.

Scary thoughts raced through the cousins' minds. It's not easy to summon the were-tiger, even if it was a family inheritance. One must make a blood sacrifice to cast an effective spell. Animal sacrifice is fine but human sacrifice is ideal. The conjuring must be done when one is naked, in the outdoors, under the full moon. Also, something vile is needed to summon the evil, which is a vial of tiger oil extracted from a tiger carcass. The master of the were-tiger also needs to feed the beast regularly with seven tiny grains of bertih rice, or puffed brown rice. Yes, the beast eats anything – chickens, cows, enemy soldiers – but this is the special food that only the master is privileged to give to his servant. It's a symbolic gesture: the were-tiger bows only to the master who feeds him the seven grains of rice. Of course, other lives are fair game.

Given the amount of effort needed to maintain a were-tiger – even a 'family' were-tiger – the cousins wondered: when did Karno find time to do this? Worryingly, *who* in the family passed this damned thing on to him?

"We're not allowed to own it, Karno, even if it's an inheritance," Suryo firmly replied. "We made a promise. That was no longer our way."

Karno, or perhaps the beast, laughed. But the laughter was quickly broken by a coughing fit. Karno leaned forward and spewed out more blood, bones and human fingers. He surveyed the mess on the floor, looked up to the horrified cousins and slowly declared: "We're not here to be victims. We're born to rule."

The irises of Karno's eyes gradually became lighter. As they turned pale yellow, the pupils narrowed and stretched into vertical slits. Residual vomit and blood dribbled down his chin. His jaw widened and his mouth stretched back to reveal fangs. Karno looked like the devil himself. Pointing his fingers – or claws – at his cousins, he said: "You people join that prophet's faith to get with the times, but it makes cows out of you. A long time ago, we were the keepers of the herd. What's wrong if I gained an eye for an eye? It was for my flesh and blood anyway."

The reference to Rahman and his son, and the old bloodline – 'the keepers of the herd' – angered my grandfather. The were-tiger didn't scare him one bit. He was barely over the death of his son Adnan, and it still weighed heavily on his mind. The wretched war, brought upon the people of Malaya by the colonisers, was none of his doing. He had made difficult choices in the past three years to save his family. And yet he couldn't save his eldest son. My grandfather certainly wasn't in the mood to listen to this wayward deviant. The anger and grief over Rahman's death wasn't Karno's alone.

"You didn't get even, Karno," my grandfather fumed, ready to drive the tas staff through Karno should the beast get provoked into an attack. "You took *seven lives*. Not two, but seven. Why kill five more? You killed because you liked it. The beast asked you for the unthinkable and you caved in to its demands. You killed more than necessary to feed the beast. You broke our code. It's a life for a life, Karno. No more, no less. You were drunk on blood."

"I gave them something to fear. I am the barrier that they will never cross again. More importantly," Karno pointed to himself, "I did something you didn't have the guts to do. I avenged my family."

"You did," my grandfather acknowledged. "In doing so, you went down to their level. Worse, you allowed yourself to become *an animal* to go down to their level. With this evil inside you, in time, you will turn on us. You've betrayed our trust in you as a keeper of the family. Repent, Karno. God is most merciful. Let this companion go."

Infuriated, Karno lunged forward to attack my grandfather. He wanted my grandfather's blood. But he was immediately thrown back to the bed, as if pushed by a mighty invisible hand. It was Suryo's spell. He could also control the were-tiger.

Suryo was much older and stronger than Karno.

"You're not getting up from the bed," Suryo said calmly. "Stay."

With that pronouncement, he pinned Karno to the bed simply with his words.

Zulfikar, who had been following silently, implored his cousin: "Karno, you're dying. You're not in a good way. You're not strong enough to take on this inheritance. Look, you even tried to kill your own cousin. That's the beast asking for your family's blood as payment. You can recover from your wound but this thing inside you isn't helping. If you don't let it go, it will consume you. Let us help you before it's too late. We've lost so much already."

Karno wept bitterly. Faith and honour come before everything else, and that's the way of the Radens. To them, what Karno did was the darkest, most evil witchcraft there was. True, the were-tiger was inherited from our ancestors since the times of the Brahman Buddhist kings. It was unleashed on the Dutch, the Portuguese, rival tribes and challengers to the throne – even relatives – to protect ourselves. But some inheritance was plain evil. It asked for the unthinkable in return for its service. The dark art has caused us a lot of pain in the past. No amount of anger and pride could justify it.

1984

So that was the story of Karno. And our grandfather. It appeared that the dark art of the were-tiger claimed Karno's sanity. His subsequent marriage improved his mental faculty.

He resumed his passion in music and played gambus with ghazal bands. But occasionally, he lapsed. As for my grandfather, he threw himself into religion, racked with guilt. His constant companion had taken human lives. It needed to be reined in.

The whole thing was a lot to digest but we let it sink in. We expected witchcraft but didn't see the were-tiger coming.

My mother broke the silence first.

"Perhaps Karno should go for a check-up. It could be Alzheimer's," she suggested.

"Perhaps," my father concurred, "Maybe it's schizophrenia. *Seeing things.* Imagining to be a tiger. This is too fantastical. We don't talk about this."

Our father worked so hard to get to where he was: a captain of Javanese ethnicity in the elite Royal Malay Regiment. The last thing he needed was another story like this that put Javanese people in a bad light. He didn't like this sort of thing. He deemed it backward.

Nobody mentioned it when our grandfather and Suryo returned from their Aidilfitri visit that evening. Our grandfather was particularly fond of Karno. He wouldn't appreciate finding out that we'd been discussing him.

That night, I had a disturbing dream. It had been three years since the constant companion appeared in my dream. Again, I was in the mist of dreaming. I was doing kick-ups with a sepak takraw ball. Or what I thought was a sepak takraw ball. Then I heard a sound. I turned my head, still bouncing the ball. It was my brother Adam. He stared at me, terrified. I grinned. "Catch!" I said, in a male voice, and passed the ball to him. He caught it with both hands and froze. It was the head of one of the soldiers who pursued the Argyll in the forest. Adam trembled. I laughed. A deep, throaty, evil laughter. Again, I had inadvertently traversed into the awful world of the constant companion. I had assumed his body in my dream and it was frightening.

I didn't tell anyone about this horrible experience. The last time I shared my nightmare with the family, my grandfather made me take a floral bath. I was already 13, mindful of my privacy, and I didn't want to go through that again.

We returned to our military camp in Kluang before the weekend approached. Adam left for his boarding school – "a creepy, haunted place," he complained – soon after.

By the end of June 1984, my father's regiment returned to Grik for their third tour of the Operation Barrier. I was very worried. As a child, I didn't understand why the Communists, who fought together with our grandfathers in World War 2, were our enemies four decades later. How was it that we, as one people, were pitted against each other because of a war that we didn't cause?

As a child of the 1980s, I was right to be confused because it was a time of contradiction. The then right-wing government launched a 'Buy British Last' campaign to boycott UK products. The 'Look East' campaign followed. The Japanese became our political ally and trade partner. They came in and taught us how to make cars. We ate Ajinomoto, and watched *Doraemon* and *Oshin* on TV.

After listening to Wak Zulfikar about World War 2, I found it all very confusing. How can light become dark, and dark become light, at the whim of fate?

I prayed for my father to return alive. I hoped God would listen to me. Secretly, I also hoped our constant companion would hear me, too.

Operation Barrier

By July 1984, my father started sending us gifts from the jungle of Grik. These included venison as tough as an old cow's hide and enormous freshwater fish so rich with fat that when grilled, the oil doused the fire instead. The taste was muddy. We tried to feed the fish to our cats. They hated it.

In August, we received a letter and more gifts in the form of game meat. In the letter was a photograph of our father and the Commanding Officer with cigarettes in their hands. The CO was standing and beside him, my father was sitting on a big wooden box, with the Grik jungle as a backdrop. My father was no smoker. We understood things were tough at the border.

The regiment returned in October 1984. He arrived home in a one-tonne army truck. My siblings and I ran outside to greet him. He hopped off from the front passenger side and limped towards us. The driver, a corporal, grinned cheekily.

"He got shot, ha!" He jested.

We were horrified. My father was expressionless. I saw that the small window on the driver's side was cracked. There was a small, round hole in the middle. It was a bullet hole.

My father said he had boils on his left thigh and bottom. At dinner time, he showed us a hole in his thigh, just above the boil. It was the size of a five-cent coin, about 5 mm deep. There was a boil there, he said. The medic cleaned it up. Was that a boil scar or did he really get hit? I never find out. But the eruption of boils was something I'd experienced before.

He told us that during the mission, his troop got ambushed whilst they were negotiating an uneven, hilly terrain. The minesweepers at the front of the flank were hit first. Then the

Quartermaster truck – his truck – got shot at. A bullet whizzed through the side window, missing our corporal's head by centimetres. The truck jolted forward as it halted. One of the front tyres rolled over a landmine. It triggered an explosion. The truck tipped over to the right side. The corporal scrambled out via the left door. The truck fell on its side, crushing two soldiers walking beside it. They died a slow, painful death. My father didn't continue his story.

What he didn't say but was later related to my mother by Lieutenant Hassan, his tennis buddy, was that, after witnessing the last rite whispered to the ears of the dying men, my father calmly picked up an M16. He got one of the snipers in the end. He aimed for the base of the man's neck and took him out cleanly and swiftly. The head and face wasn't damaged at all. He made sure the body wasn't despoiled and was good for identification – in line with the Geneva Convention. Hassan said he'd never seen my father like that. He'd won second or third prizes before in shooting competitions, which meant our father was average. This level of efficiency wasn't expected of him at all. After this incident, he fell ill with 'jungle fever'. Painful, large boils erupted on his body.

It took a few months before my father returned to his usual self. When his mood finally improved, he entertained us with stories of wild animals and how the soldiers hunted for food. The wild jungle cattle – frightening to both humans and tigers – had to be shot from a boat in the river. The giant snakehead fish snacked on monkeys – when they fell into the river – or human fingers, if humans were careless enough to dip their hands into the water. Yes, the fish tasted awful.

We also found out later that, apart from the ambush earlier in the mission, my father's troop didn't engage with the enemies as much. The Communists got the message and cleared off. The focus was on the minesweepers to clean up the area until their mission ended.

But there was this one evening in September when they heard growls outside their encampment. "Ok, who the fuck complained about Grandpa Tiger this time?" The soldiers asked each other. There's this superstition about what not to do when in the jungle: never say bad things about the wild beasts. Elephants, tigers – they're off-limits. Do that and you will get a visit. It happened to the soldiers in the past – with an irate elephant. But that's another story.

The soldiers decided that there was a tiger on the loose. They were warned not to drift too far away from base camp, and to never mobilise alone. Nobody left the encampment at night.

A few nights later, they heard screams in the distance. It came from the heart of the jungle, on the hill above them. Again, they heard the familiar growls. "Was it the Communists?" They asked each other. The human screams escalated into cries of desperation, pain and terror, almost animal-like. The soldiers whispered to each other: "*Is something bad happening to them?*". They decided that it was best not to leave their site. There are mightier, more formidable beings than men in the jungle, and it's best not to throw one's weight around.

The soldiers waited until daybreak to investigate. Three went into the jungle to recce and returned with a grim piece of news: they found two dead enemy combatants. There were blood and guts everywhere. The injuries were so horrific it made the soldiers tremble. Did they venture into a territory where no humans should enter? Naturally, it was the Quartermaster's duty to oversee the collection of the remains.

My father and three of his men went over to pick up the bodies, accompanied by the soldiers who discovered the remains. Looking at the bodies, one would be forgiven to think that they got blown to pieces by landmines. But there was no landmine in the area. The Quartermaster men tied the hands and feet of each body to a stick. Each body was then carried by two soldiers, one in front and one at the back. My father was one of the men in front.

As they travelled downhill to the base camp, the dead man's feet, bound together, pressed repeatedly against my father's shoulder. The deceased's intestine trailed on the grass. It gave my father the creeps. But the Geneva Convention had to be adhered to. Bodies of combatants had to be returned to their families, once identified. And yet nobody really knew how they died. It was convenient to put in the record that they got attacked by a tiger.

The visitation

In 2010, I was working on a paper on colonial education policy in British Malaya for an anthropology seminar when I came across an unexpected nugget at the library of the School of Oriental and African Studies in London. It was a book written by one of the former governors posted in the Straits Settlement.

I do find it curious that quite a few of the colonial administrators in the settlements took a keen, if not unhealthy, interest in our shamanism and witchcraft. They knew it wasn't a very progressive subject – in fact, frowned upon by the natives themselves – but it didn't stop the likes of R.O. Winstedt and R. J. Wilkinson from having a gander and devoting books on it.

This nugget, not related at all to the policy I was researching on, was a book published in 1916, written by Sir Hugh Clifford, a prominent British Resident who later became the Governor of North Borneo. He called it "The Were-Tiger", based on his experience in Malaya administering one of the East Coast states.

I read his 'fictionalised' account of a were-tiger massacre of a family and recognised the similarities between that incident and the one Wak Zulfikar described to us way back in 1984 when I was a child. I'm not superstitious, my father even less so. But Clifford's story made me wonder about the 1945 incident. I enjoyed the historical bit, but the eerie bit... Well, my grandfather said nothing to corroborate it.

Being the vanguard of a colonial project that saw us moved from superstition and feudalism to a constitutional monarchy, Clifford, oddly enough, seemed keener to discuss the phenomenon. But he was but a curious outsider, not weighed down by an unwanted legacy. We, on the other hand, are inseparable from our constant companion, and are desperate to deny its existence.

Perhaps it was the amount of coffee consumed, or the volume of information digested for my research paper, but that evening, for the first time in two decades, the constant companion came to me in my dream.

The good thing was I didn't assume his body in the dreaming, unlike before. I saw him standing before me – a tall man with long hair, knotted partly in a bun, with the rest cascading over his shoulder down to his bare chest – fidgeting over a silver ring on one of his fingers. I recognised it to be Hagar's ring. We were in a jewellery shop in Lisbon, Portugal, on a holiday when she bought it.

"What are you doing with that ring?" I demanded.

"I like it," he replied. He showed the ring to me. "Barongan," he said. *A bear.*

"It doesn't belong to you."

"It's a down payment."

"For what?"

The constant companion looked at me and said nothing.

The dream stopped abruptly at that point and I woke up to find myself, thankfully, in London. I looked out the window to see ash trees and their leaves glimmering in the autumn sunlight. On the dresser next to my bed was an ikebana arrangement of blue thistles and blades of grass. My sister Hagar had been decorating our flat with her floral 'universes' after every ikebana lesson. It was autumn so she experimented on thistles lately. The grass made me sneeze but I felt reassured to see the floral composition by my bedside.

But a week later, Hagar complained that her ring had gone missing.

"Sarah, did you see the silver ring we bought in Lisbon on our holiday?" She asked.

"Which one?" I said. "There are a few."

"The one with the teddy bear."

"How long has it been missing for?"
"A few days. Did you see it anywhere in the flat?"
I deliberated. Then I replied: "No."
In our earthly realm, I didn't. In another world, yes.
I expected some news to arrive from home. The constant companion has a habit of returning when trouble is afoot.

THE NIGHT
OF THE
FLYING
BLADES

The maternal bloodline

The Al-Jaffari Family Tree

Merong Mahawangsa
Founder of Langkasuka
Period of reign: c.100 CE

The dawn of the northern kingdoms
of Nakhon Si Thammarat & Kedah
circa 100 CE

TWO OF THE EIGHT DESCENDANTS

Hindu-Buddhist Malay kingdoms
of Perak, Kedah, Kelantan &
Terengganu
circa 100 CE

King Ganji Sarjuna
Founder of Gangga Negara
Period of reign: c.100 CE

King Ong Maha Perita Deria
The Fanged King (deposed)
Period of reign: c.100 CE

Syed Hassan
Al-Jaffari   married   Princess Seroja

The arrival of the Syeds
The decline of Hindu-Buddhist kingdoms
circa 1500s

Samad son of Abdullah   Siti Puteh
(Wangli or Onglee)   Al-Jaffari
        married

The Larut Wars
British ascendancy
1861-1890

Wan Halimah (Moyang)

Siam handed over the northern
Malay kingdoms to the British
Formation of British Malaya
1890-1930

Syed Mokhtar   Wan Hashimah (Opah)
Al-Jaffari   married

Siti Puteh   Syed Alwi   Siti Nora   Captain Raden
b. 1960   1955   b. 1950   b. 1942
                    married

World War 2
1939-1945
The Malayan Emergency
1948-1960

Adam   Sarah   Hagar   Maryam
1969 - 2005   b. 1972   b. 1973   b. 1975

The Communist insurgency
1960-1989

The keeper of my mother's kin

This is the story of the keeper of my mother's kin. The last we heard of the flying keris was after the war. There was a demon that wielded the blade, but no human eyes could see it, it's said. The flying blades are justice reserved for those betrayed by kith and kin. Given the damages inflicted on the enemies, it's not likely that the keeper will be summoned again. It made everyone frightened of us. But we still have traitors in our midst. Sometimes fear is the only thing that gets through to them.

A bad excursion

Treason comes from within.

Magic, they say, is what science can't explain. Then what I'm about to tell you might as well be magic. I had witnessed something extraordinary in my childhood and was later told it was never what I thought it was.

In 1985, four years before the Communists laid down their weapons following the Hat Yai Treaty, the Kluang military camp where we lived had begun to train paramilitary newbies. These were new recruits from the Malaysian Volunteer Corps Department. In the past, under the British, they were known as Home Guards or HGs. Their job was to be the eyes and the ears within our third line of defence. In other words, to help the military and police forces keep things in check. They were given weapons. They had power to arrest. But they were civilians.

Kluang, the small town less than 200 km away from Singapore, was already a thriving halfway hub in the south of Peninsula Malaysia. Switch on the TV and you'd think we were in the West. The new private TV channel, TV3, broadcasts *Dynasty* and *MTV*. The old government station, Radio TV Malaysia, showed *Dallas*. Singapore Broadcasting Corporation showed *Sesame Street* in the afternoon, all sorts of American mini-series in the evening and yes, *Solid Gold*. The Indonesian radio station next door played UK and US rock hits. Hong Kong comedy and martial art films dominated the cinema.

There was simply no room for Communist propaganda in the mind of a 14-year-old. I wanted to be as cool as Cyndi Lauper, although I know my father would shoot me dead if I had her haircut.

My father, a captain in the Royal Malay Regiment, wasn't that scary of a man. But he did have an opinion on the crops of volunteers the camp received periodically for training. He found the young men a bit disrespectful and the women too forward for his liking.

One day, he came home from work grumbling: "I saw two female volunteers in drainpipe jeans eating ice cream *whilst walking back* to their barrack." Looking at his face, you could imagine what he'd seen: two women, red lipsticks, permed hair piled high and propped up with hair gel and hairspray, and camel-toe denims. "Children," he warned, "Don't you ever let me catch you doing that."

There were still four children in the family in 1985: my older brother Adam, myself, my sister Hagar and the youngest, Sarah. Adam passed away almost two decades later. Whilst he was alive, he was the keeper of his siblings in more ways than you could imagine.

Saturday, 9 February 1985

January was a drag, awash with rain. The new year period got a bit interesting when, in early February 1985, during the weekend before Valentine's Day, my father got a phone call from the military police. It was about 7.30 pm. We were about to sit down for dinner at home. One of the female volunteers got struck down by hysteria. It took three female soldiers to hold her down; it was that rough. My father took his torchlight and picked up the keys to his blue Peugeot. Before he left, he said to our mother: "Leave some dinner for me. Make sure the rice is warm." I watched him at the door as he drove off. Our home in the officers' quarter, about a kilometre from the foot of Mount Lambak, was some 3 km away from the privates' barracks.

We were already in bed when my father came home late at night. I didn't get the full story until the day after. When we woke up, he'd already left for work. We returned from high school, after being picked up by an army truck. As the four of us piled into the kitchen in search of food, we overheard my father's batman, Nik, talking to our mother.

"Two privates held down her arms, one each. One pinned down her legs to stop her thrashing about. She swore and spat at everyone."

"Who swore and spat at everyone?" My brother Adam asked.

"The female volunteer who was hysterical last night," Nik replied in his singsong Kelantanese accent.

We took our place at the kitchen table, eager to hear more.

"Captain Raden was greeted by a female Warrant Officer

when he arrived at the ladies' barrack. I arrived on my Vespa minutes later, at about 7.50 pm. The volunteers told us she got into hysterics not long after everyone returned from dinner. We were figuring out what to do when suddenly she pushed off the privates holding her down. Just like that. The woman sat up in bed, her back straight, put her palms together like this--," Nik pressed his palms together as if praying, "-- and spoke in garbled Sanskrit. Or something similar."

"How do you know it was Sanskrit?" my mother asked, surprised.

"It sounds like one of the prayers you hear via a loudspeaker at a Buddhist temple," Nik said. He briefly mimicked the incoherent murmuring of a Buddhist chant to illustrate his point. "There are quite a few of those in Kelantan, where I came from."

We almost forgot that Nik's village was from south of the border of Thailand.

Nik continued: "She looked almost like... a Buddhist monk praying. But she looked scary. Not friendly like a monk. The voice wasn't hers. The face..." Nik paused to shudder. "She was *possessed*."

Here we go again, I thought. Ghostly possession.

"Do you think it's Captain John?" Adam asked, looking perturbed. Captain John was the nickname the soldiers at the camp gave to the headless British soldier – a ghost that, for a short while, scared the living daylights out of us two years ago. It happened during the exhumation of the remains of 'Gurkha' soldiers two years before. Well, we had assumed those were Gurkhas but we were wrong.

"Captain John wouldn't have spoken in Sanskrit," Nik said. He went on:

> "The possessed woman got carted off to the military hospital where she was sedated and looked after. Moments after the ambulance picked her up, Captain Raden asked the two military policemen to step out of the barrack. He said he had a few questions to ask the women. The MPs understood.

They gave him 20 minutes and temporarily left.

"Captain Raden then asked the volunteers if any of them smoked pot. He reassured them they won't get reported to the police. The penalty for drug trafficking is severe. If you get caught with a stash weighing around the weight of three 20 sen coins, you're done for. It's the death penalty. So he knew not to scare them. One or two ladies confessed. They said one of the male volunteers got a small stash. Captain Raden told them they're not qualified to be volunteers if they consume intoxicants such as spliff. He reprimanded them for that.

"One of the women said:

'We didn't do any of these during our training. She got in a state hours after we came back from our weekend excursion.'

'What type of excursion?' Captain Raden asked.

'We got taken to the Yap Village and the farming areas nearby.'

"Yap is one of the New Villages created by the British to relocate displaced Chinese communities after the Second World War. It's about 4 km south of our camp, in the shadow of Mount Lambak. The woman told us they were on a tour to see the living quarters, the plantations, the chicken farms and the local Buddhist temple.

'A Buddhist temple?' Captain Raden asked. 'Why did you do that?'

'It was a tour.'

'It's a place of worship. Members of the Malaysian Volunteer Corps Department or the military can't just go there. We have to respect the communities' space. It's not under surveillance.'

'The people at the temple didn't mind, though. The monks said it was fine'.

"Another woman interjected: 'Yeah, we didn't do anything bad. Just took photos and stuff.'

'Did you have their permission to take pictures?'
Captain Raden inquired, looking very serious.

"The woman looked guilty.

'Not really. The monks said no photos,' the other
woman chimed in quietly.

'Let me guess,' Captain Raden said, 'They left you
alone and you guys took photos of the temple.'

"The women reluctantly nodded. The other
volunteers also nodded their heads. Captain Raden
didn't look happy.

'Where are the photos?' He asked.

'Being developed at one of the photography shops
in town,' said the woman who first spoke of the
excursion.

"Captain Raden turned around to me and said:
'Nik, I want you to pick up those photos when they're
ready. Get the receipts from these women,' he
ordered.

'Yes, sir,' I responded, saluting him.

'And the male volunteers, too,' he added.

'Yes, sir!'.

"Seconds later, we heard knocks on the door. The
female Warrant Officer let the MPs in. Our 20
minutes of privacy with the volunteers were up.

'All good here?' Asked one of them.

Yes,' Captain Raden replied, 'All good.'

"Before we parted ways that evening, Captain
Raden said to me: 'Nik, I think there's more to this
than just a visit to the Buddhist temple.'

'In what sense, sir?'

'Do you know the areas the volunteers patrol as
part of their two-week training here?'

'The Chinese villages. Yap Village is one of them.
The plantations.'

'Night or daytime patrol?'

'Night, I think.'

"With that, he let me off. I saluted him, got on my

Vespa and headed back to my barrack."

Whilst our father was getting to the bottom of things at the camp, he decided to send us away from the military camp for the Lunar New Year holiday. The national holiday was from Wednesday, 20 February 1985 to Thursday, 21 February 1985. School was shut for a week from the Saturday before the Lunar New Year. Our father thought Kluang was getting too westernised. There were enough bad elements to corrupt us. The incident of hysteria at the volunteer barrack convinced him so.

Because he could only leave on Wednesday and not before, our father asked our mother's brother Syed Alwi — a member of the Royal Rangers Regiment — to come and pick us up that Saturday.

First, our uncle dropped Adam and I off at our paternal grandfather's home in Merlimau, Malacca. Then, he drove the rest — my mother and my two younger sisters — up to our maternal grandmother's place in Sitiawan, Perak, a further 300 km away up north.

Lucky them. They didn't have to witness what we witnessed at our grandfather's place.

88

The Popsicle man

Sunday, 17 February 1985

It was only after the rest of the family left for Perak that my grandparents informed Adam and I of the situation brewing at home.

"My cousins, Suryo and Karno, are staying with us for a few days," my grandfather said. Adam and I looked at each other. Karno the *crazy* uncle? The one who thought he was some kind of were-tiger?

"Just for a few days," my grandmother reassured us.

"To what end?" Adam asked suspiciously.

"Salma!" My grandmother bellowed, beckoning at our aunt, my father's sister. "Why don't you make these kids some tea and fry them some crisps?"

She ignored Adam's question. Something was up.

"Where's Atan and Amat?" She asked, referring to Aunt Salma's younger sons, who were ten and seven in age.

"By the fish pond."

My grandfather perked up. "Get them away from the pond," he said. "Suryo and Karno are coming. Nobody strayed outside after evening prayer."

My grandfather's home in Merlimau was a typical Malaccan home: wooden, dark brown in colour, lovely tall windows with ornate coloured glass panels on top that let the sunlight in. The whole house was about 30 m in length, from end to end.

The West wing, where the hearth, the kitchen, the wide dining area and the bathroom were located, was on the ground floor. The East wing, which housed the other half of the house, was elevated some 1.5 m from the ground. This elevated wooden construction was on wooden stilts. This was where the bedrooms, the living room and the visitor's hall were located.

To get from the West wing to the elevated unit of the East wing, one had to climb a set of wooden stairs from the dining area.

The main entrance, a big wooden door with two panels, was located on the East Wing. This imposing entrance faced the flower garden and a small earth path that fed into the main road. A massive, glazed earthenware jar, a tempayan, sat next to the stairs that led up to the main entrance. It was filled with water. In it, two gourami fishes swam around. The water was used to wash our feet before we entered the house. It was important to have clean feet because shoes aren't allowed in homes.

This house, together with the neighbouring homes, made up the dwelling area that lined the River Kesang.

To get to my grandfather's house, you'd have to walk some 30m from the main road. You'd have to cross a tiny bridge over the river — so narrow it often got mistaken for a wide monsoon drain. You'd also have to cross a small wooden plank over a very tiny stream to enter the front garden. This was actually the brook that fed into the fish pond. My grandfather dug this fish pond himself decades ago.

In the past, chickens were kept under the house. When my father received his generous army bonus, he paid for the wooden house to be repainted black, and the space under the house to be fenced. The chickens no longer lived under the house.

Over the years, my grandfather built his home to slowly resemble the Cirebon keraton, the Javanese royal court he grew up in. It wasn't as big, of course, but gave an air of gentility. He built the fish pond in front of the West wing so that he could enjoy the view whilst having tea.

The front garden was decorated with flower plants such as hibiscus, ixora chinensis and roses. The backyard was an orchard. In this orchard was another pond deeper than the fish pond. The family used to bathe here before the bathroom was built.

There were plenty of fruit trees such as pomelo, mango, rambutan and rose apples. The chickens and goats resided in the orchard.

Looking at the area, you wouldn't have guessed what happened between 1942 and 1945 here. No traces of atrocities survived in villages like this. But that doesn't mean evil isn't lurking about.

Suryo and Karno arrived in the late afternoon, in time for tea and crisps. Suryo, the older of the two cousins, was robust in his build, slightly rounded and cheerful in his disposition. He had a pair of thick-rimmed spectacles on and wore a Javanese headgear in batik. He was a farmer but in his spare time, Suryo was also a bomoh. Or a shaman, as Westerners call it. Karno, the youngest of the five Cirebon cousins, was thin, sullen and quieter in demeanour. Nothing about the way Karno dressed distinguished him from the Malays. He looked just like a local.

All of us – my grandparents, his two cousins, Adam, Aunt Salma, the two little boys and I – sat in a circle on a big mat laid on the floor of the living room. Tea, crisps and biscuits were placed in the middle. The smell of cloves and cinnamon wafted through the air. "It smelled delicious," I complimented, as I reached out for a biscuit.

My grandmother made a face. The two boys sank their fingers into their mother's arms. They looked scared.

My grandfather explained the situation to us:

"The house has been smelling of kretek cigarettes for weeks. No one here smokes. I've given up smoking ages ago because of my heart. The smell just got worse and worse. You can even pick it up now.

"Two weeks ago, Atan woke up in the middle of the night to go to the bathroom. The boys sleep with me in the back bedroom. He woke me up. I told him to switch on the light and move along. Minutes later, he came back running and screaming: 'I saw a ghost! I saw a ghost!'.

"I thought: What on earth? I got up, picked up my cane and walked to the kitchen. Atan was behind me the whole time. The area smelled of kretek cigarettes. In fact, there was smoke wafting about. Very unusual. 'Who's there?' I shouted, thinking we had an intruder. By this time, Salma arrived at the kitchen. She was woken up by the noise.

"I asked Atan: 'Who did you see?'.

'A ghost,' he shrieked.

'What ghost?'

'I saw a man sitting there,' he said, pointing to a small wooden chair in the kitchen, steps away from the bathroom. 'He sat with one leg up on the chair, smoking a cigarette. He wore a white T-shirt and a pair of black baggy shorts. His face looks like one of the masked men in the TV ad.'

'Masked? TV ad?' I asked, confused by it all.

'Ice cream TV ad. The Popsicle hero was chased by indigenous people who wore scary monster masks. Like lions. Or bears. His face is like that.'

'Have you been watching too much telly?' Salma asked.

'Hush,' I said to Salma. 'What about this monster man? You saw him smoking there? What else did you see?'

'His neck was cut open…'

'What??'

'His neck was cut open with the veins and blood coming out of it. When he exhaled, smoke came out of his neck. It smelled like kretek.'

"I looked at Atan, I looked at Salma, and I looked at the kretek smoke still wafting in the air. If the boy had been lying, I'd have given him a good hiding. But I could tell he wasn't lying. He was absolutely terrified.

"The following day, I called Suryo. I described what happened.

'It's gotten more brazen,' Suryo said.

'Or careless,' I said. 'It let itself be seen, most likely by mistake.'

"We both agreed this has gone on too long. Something has to be done. It's starting to disturb my grandson and I won't have this."

Adam and I looked at each other, baffled. Gone on too long? We wondered what that meant. Was this so-called the constant companion, the otherworldly servant of our family who kept appearing where he shouldn't?

"In case you're wondering," Suryo said, as if he'd read our minds, "This isn't one of ours."

"Then whose?" Adam asked.

"Someone who has something against your grandparents – or us – for quite some time. This is the most extreme it's been."

"We don't know who," my grandfather said, "But we will return this demon to its master. Then hopefully we'll find out who the person is. We'll know when it hounds the master at his own home."

"And why he is doing this to us," my grandmother said.

The exorcism took place that same evening after evening prayer. The windows and doors were shut. Again, we all sat in a circle on the floor in the living room. Karno placed a small brass bowl with burning incense in the middle. Next to it, he placed a bowl of water with slices of lime floating.

Suryo and Karno did a special prayer whilst we watched. Suryo stared into the bowl of water. I reckoned he wasn't really looking at the bowl but at something else that we couldn't see.

"Where is your tiang seri?" He asked my grandfather. He meant the main pillar of the house. This is the heart of every traditional Malay or Javanese home.

"Over there, next to my wife's bedroom. The TV is there."

"When was the last time you gave that area a good dusting?"

"Salma would have cleaned that area yesterday."

"You missed out something. Or rather, it's well hidden."

"What is well hidden?"

"One of the spells."

We gasped. Suryo whispered to Karno in Javanese. Karno nodded, got up and walked to the main wooden pillar past our grandmother's bedroom. He returned with a small, dark, worn-out pouch. "I found this at the top of the pillar," he said. Karno sat down, opened the pouch and poured the content out. A piece of paper, neatly folded into a tiny square, fell out. Suryo picked it up. He unfolded it. It was a piece torn off a page of the Quran. He read it and shook his head.

"Animal!" My grandfather cursed. He was angry that the holy words were used for such evil deeds.

"This has been on the pillar for about ten years," Suryo calmly explained. "It's the most recent spell sent to your home. Maybe the last one. I believe the sender is already dead."

"Well, that's a comfort," my grandfather replied

sarcastically. "Are there more?"

"Yes. An older one. That may have been around longer than a decade." Suryo looked intently into the bowl of water. "It's hidden underground. No. It's below the water surface."

My grandfather sighed. He knew something that we didn't.

"I think I know where it is," he murmured.

"It's in the fish pond," Suryo revealed. He looked up to scan our worried faces. "We have to remove it tonight but it's well guarded. Which means we can't see it with our own eyes. Karno will help me remove it. But," he paused for a moment, "I have to remove my clothes. Only when I'm naked, I can see where it is in the pond."

"Not in front of the children," my grandmother protested.

"No, no. Only Karno and I will go to the pond to look for it," Suryo reassured her.

"How are you going to remove it?" My grandfather asked.

"Karno will accompany me to the fish pond. I'll strip and hand over my clothes to him. He'll light up the area using the torchlight. I'll wade into the pool to retrieve that sodding thing." The two cousins got up, and walked to the front door. The rest of us followed behind. They turned around to face us.

"The rest of you stay inside," Suryo said. "Make sure you lock the doors. Don't open until we tell you so."

My grandfather locked the door after them. Adam went to the nearest window. He peeked through the curtain. In the distance, we heard the cousins say their prayers. Not long after, we heard the sound of water splashing. Suryo had gone into the fish pond. We heard more sounds of water stirring. Five minutes of this and then silence. After a while, a cry rang out: "I found it!". It was Suryo.

There were sounds of jubilation, of excited chatter. But suddenly, this celebratory noise was cut short by loud shouting. We heard two people yelling at each other. The verbal exchange wasn't in Malay. We leaned towards the door to listen carefully. It wasn't in Javanese either. *Oh no.* It wasn't Suryo and Karno. The voices sounded gruff – guttural in their speech and at times animal-like.

"Ahmad!" Suryo called out. "Open the door! Open the door!"

"Suryo! Karno!" My grandfather cried as he unlocked the door.

The sounds of footsteps got louder and louder as the cousins streaked to the main entrance. The yelling, in the meantime, intensified, accompanied by the sound of violent splashes.

My grandfather quickly opened the door. Karno burst in. Suryo stumbled behind, wearing only a sarong around his waist. In the rush, he left his clothes behind. For a split second, we saw — or we thought we saw — a keris and a machete clashing forcefully above the fish pond. They appeared to be flying in the air. But there was no time to digest what we had seen. Suryo shouted: "Close the door!". My grandfather shut the door, pressing it firmly with both hands.

There were loud bangs. It was as if two people were brawling and throwing each other against the walls of the house. The fight had reached us. The scuffle ended at the west wing of the house, outside the kitchen. Someone — or something — kicked the kitchen door several times. The wooden walls vibrated.

"You dare!" Suryo shouted towards the kitchen. "You dare do that!". His rebuke was reciprocated with a shout. The language was unintelligible to us. Suryo hastily turned to look at my grandfather. "Ahmad, step away from the door!" He cried. My grandfather stepped back, in time to avoid the tip of a machete that suddenly penetrated through the wooden door. "God forgive us!" My grandfather cried in surprise.

There were more sounds: boxing, kicking, swearing and blades clashing. And then, silence.

"He left," Adam quietly said. He stepped away from the window.

"You *saw* him?" Suryo asked, looking at Adam with disbelief.

"I did," Adam confirmed. "He chased it away." My brother

turned to look at Atan. "He chased away your Popsicle man."

My grandfather, Suryo and Karno were stunned. They didn't expect this from Adam. My brother did tell me he'd seen that strange friend around. The Constant Companion was invisible to me – except in my nightmares. Still, I had no idea what was going on at that moment. It sounded crazy but this was what I had seen that night: some fucking blades whizzing in the air, all by themselves.

My grandfather opened the front door to find the machete buried on the other side of it. He cursed in Javanese as he yanked it out. A keris was stuck on a wooden pillar at the front porch. It was long, the undulating blade about 30 cm in length. The handle looked like it was made of ivory, with the tip covered in gold. It looked very old.

Karno went to the pillar and removed the keris. He produced a wooden sheath from his pocket and slipped the blade inside. Karno turned around to find me standing by the door, staring at the weapon in disbelief. He concealed the weapon in the waist of his trouser and walked past as if it wasn't a big deal.

The keris was our family heirloom. Along with the constant companion.

We returned to the living room, back to the mat on the floor. Again, we sat in a circle, but this time huddling together out of fear. Karno added more incense into the brass bowl.

Suryo produced a small plastic carrier bag. He took out what looked like a black pouch, slightly larger than the one Karno found earlier on the main pillar of the house. He carefully picked up the corner of the pouch. It was actually a folded piece of cloth made of cotton pelikat fabric. This fabric is customarily worn by men.

"Pelikat fabric?" Aunt Salma questioned. "That size?"

"It's the size of a pelikat cut-out we used for menstruation," my grandmother pointed out. "The kind of old rag we repurposed before sanitary pads existed."

"Mother, you're right," Aunt Salma concurred.

"That's disgusting," I said.

"Typical hexing stuff," said Suryo.

"What's inside?" Aunt Salma probed.

"Well, let's see… Oh. A *monkey*'s skull?"

We looked at the darkened, crumbling macaque skull that Suryo unveiled. It was very small, no bigger than a toddler's fist. But still, it was macabre. The fucker decapitated a baby macaque and used the head as part of the spell.

"Karno, could you please give me your ballpen?" Suryo politely asked. Karno handed over his pen to his cousin. Suryo poked around the skull.

"You see this?" Suryo held up a tiny, green plastic toy soldier about 4 cm in height. It was one of those common plastic freebies found in crisp packages. There was something odd, however, about the toy soldier. There was a dark, long nail that was bent around its crotch.

"What does this mean?" My grandmother demanded.

"A nail around the crotch? Is it a spell to break up our marriages?" Aunt Salma asked.

"Not sure," Suryo sighed. He looked at my grandfather. "It's over now. We'll get rid of this."

"Suryo, how long has it been in the pond?" My grandfather asked.

"A long time."

"The toy soldier. Is that meant to be my father?" Adam asked.

We stopped and stared at him. Suddenly I felt frightened. My father. The soldier. Was this spell also meant to bring harm to my father?

"Your father is protected," Karno reassured us. "No harm will come his way."

Suryo and my grandfather flinched. I could tell they were

disturbed by Karno's statement. To this day, I wasn't sure if the bit about Karno being the family were-tiger was true. But who am I to question? Or decline help when it's needed?

"Let's burn these straight away," my grandfather hastily said. "We say our night prayer afterwards." He was eager to get this behind us – and to avoid discussing what Karno said.

The rage of the Red Sash

Monday, 18 February 1985

The following afternoon, at teatime, I asked my grandfather's cousins about the keris. Specifically on its ability to fly. The night before, I heard noises but I didn't really see any blades flying with my own eyes. So I told myself. Adam made a face at me but the rest of the family didn't seem perturbed by my curiosity. My grandmother poured tea for us whilst we anticipated the answer from Suryo and Karno.

Suryo said flying keris wasn't a new thing. Local people had had the flying blades out particularly during the Malayan Emergency period, when the Malayan Communist Party terrorised the people after the Second World War.

The Communists were snakes, the thorn in the British side, Suryo explained. During that war, they joined forces with the Allied to form Force 136 to fight the Japanese occupiers. But as everyone suspected, the Communists squirrelled away 'lost consignments' and weapons from the battlefield that the Allied parachuted into the jungles.

They terrorised Malaya in the two weeks after the Japanese surrender in August 1945. They occupied police stations and flew their hammer-and-sickle flags. They executed Japanese soldiers and suspected collaborators after organising their own kangaroo courts. Some were innocent and just happened to be at the wrong place and the wrong time.

The British returned and demanded them to give up their weapons. They did. But they had plenty stashed away.

What turned the local villagers against the Communists in that two-week period was the curfew they imposed. They went over to Muar, the district next to us where Karno and Suryo lived. They told people to stay indoors. The town residents, easily contained, had no choice but to adhere.

It was harder in the remote villages where the Javanese communities lived. The Communists told them not to leave the area – not even for Friday prayer. That was the death knell. You don't say that to those Javanese. They weren't exactly uneducated peasants. They were farmers who hailed from keratons, like my grandfather's cousins.

The Javanese mobilised. Several vigilante squads were formed. There were no guns available to the farmers, so they used farming equipment such as sickles, machetes and makeshift spears.

They also deployed extra ammunition: the flying blades. It was white witchery, but still, *witchery*. The farmers put on red sashes over their black clothes and called themselves "Selepang Merah" – the Red Sash. They became the most fearsome vigilante.

In time, they, too, became a source of concern for the authorities. But things were wild in those two weeks in August 1945. The British, still limping from the war, had taken time to regroup. They couldn't protect anyone at that stage.

"Did they win against the Communists?" I asked Suryo.

"We did," Karno replied out of the blue.

"Were you a Red Sash?" I gasped.

"I was," Karno confirmed, his face sullen.

Suryo broke into a smile. Cryptically, he said: "Karno was all things he *shouldn't have been*."

I blinked back, puzzled. "What happened to the Red Sash?" I probed.

"The Red Sash got disbanded," Suryo replied. "The British returned and things stabilised."

"But we paid a price," Karno stressed. He sighed heavily. He proceeded to recount the tragic story of Kepong Hill – barely an hour away from our village – where the lives brutally lost finally convinced the locals to cooperate with the British.

The Kepong Hill massacre

1950

"Everyone knew the Communists would turn against us at any time, judging from the evil they were capable of in those two weeks after the Japanese surrender. We wanted our country back," Karno told us.

"The British, knowing full well they were birds of passage, had outlined a plan to pave the way for our independence. But the Communists wanted more. They wanted all of our country. Locals who supported them during the war initially backed them.

"Some of the impoverished Chinese, driven to live in squatters at the edge of the jungles during the war, joined the Min Yuen – the undercover, laymen branch of the Malayan Communist Party – to be moles, to supply food and so on. However, the Communists' tendency to disrupt civilian life – not only the British armed personnel – gradually turned everyone against them.

"In 1946, Sir Edward Gent was appointed the Governor of the Malayan Union. His objective was to continue the unpopular plan hatched before the war kicked off, which was to reduce the Rulers to mere figureheads, and to turn us into a Republic. It was a big mistake. People were upset.

"By this time, the situation was ripe for volatility. The Communists took advantage. They weren't in the doghouse yet, fresh from being a Force 136 collaborator. But they did what snakes do. Behind everyone's back, they infiltrated labour unions. They shadowed youth associations.

"In 1947, there were hundreds of strikes, mainly in rubber plantations, fanned by the Communists. Naturally, kongsi groups were formed yet again to mobilise against the Communists.

"So the British, the planters and the locals had two problems on their hands: the antagonistic Communists, and the antagonistic kongsi groups formed to fend off the Communists.

"The British acted by introducing a legislation that banned those convicted with blackmails, intimidations and whatnot from holding union positions. That, at last, sorted out the Communists' grip on labour unions.

"This was when the Communists recruited former members of the Japanese war resistance as Min Yuen. Weapons previously hidden away were distributed to the Min Yuen. Many joined voluntarily. But many also got blackmailed into joining. It was a murky time.

"In the middle of June 1948, the Communists mobilised in earnest. They shot dead a British estate manager at his office desk. This happened at the River Siput in Kuala Kangsar, Perak. It was 8.30 am. Half an hour later, the Communists killed another British estate manager and his assistant at an estate a mile away. Elsewhere, a Chinese contractor was murdered in Perak. Another Chinese contractor in Johore was also murdered. The British declared a State of Emergency to the entire country.

"Here, what really turned us against the Communists was the massacre of Kepong Hill. It was 23 February 1950. About 200 terrorists surrounded 13 Malay policemen and their families at the remote police station. They emptied rounds of bullets on the station. They set it on fire.

"The policemen knew they couldn't win. They

knew their beloved families would perish. They did what we'd do in that situation. They charged at the Communists, some with their clothes still burning. They were shot dead. Their wives, who ran behind their husbands closely, took up the guns and started shooting. A few were shot dead. One was caught.

"She was frogmarched to the married quarters by the Communists. They instructed her to call on the wives and children in the quarters to surrender. She said there was only a woman and her daughter left. There was no point in doing so. The Communists shot her dead. Then they called the poor lady and her daughter to come out. The lady said she'd rather die. The Communists set the married quarters on fire, burning both of them alive.

"Afterwards, they found a boy, the son of one of the dead policemen, hiding in an underground bunker. They dragged him out, kicking and screaming, and threw him into one of the burning buildings alive. They gathered the injured policemen. They, too, were thrown into the fire alive.

"The charred bodies were found the following day by ten men of the jungle squad, who were accompanied by several men from the Seaforth Highlanders. They arrived at the top of the hill to find a scene of utter devastation. The survivors, women and children who managed to hide away from the Communists, were found howling, crying for their loved ones.

"And you'd think the Malays would appreciate the sacrifice of these men and women. No. Until now, the fundamentalist Islamic pricks have circulated rumours about the policemen drinking and gambling to celebrate Chinese New Year. Goodness, they were Malays! Plus, Chinese New Year didn't fall on 23 February. Rather, a week before, on 17 February 1950.

"It's unbelievable that they try to sully the memory of our heroes. Naturally, tensions were high in the aftermath of the massacre. The locals were more than willing to exact revenge on the innocent local Chinese population.

"Fortunately, the police regiment stopped them. The villagers were informed that one of the masterminds behind the Kepong Hill massacre was a Malay. A man by the name of Mat Indera."

Our mouths fell open. The traitor was one of our kind. Just like the man who attempted to send my grandfather to Burma during the Japanese occupation.

"What made it worse was that he was from Batu Pahat, not miles away from here," Suryo contextualised. "That pissed off the locals greatly."

"Why did he do that to his own kind?" I asked, bewildered.

"God knows," Suryo replied. "He went to a religious school. He was a man of faith. But he turned Communist during the war. Mat Indera was active in the labour movement when he was a coolie in Singapore. That much we know."

"There were also those who were unhappy that we had former Japanese soldiers living amongst us after the war," my grandfather added. "These were young men – boys, rather – who refused to return after war. They became Malays. They became one of us. *Saudara baru*. So we were obliged to protect them. But because of this, the Communists accused us of siding with the Japanese during the war. This is so untrue."

We fell silent for a while. I was reminded of the story of Yamashiro Ryu. The former boy soldier whom we all called Pak Arshad. He ran a bicycle shop in town. He fixed my bicycle once. Funny but I never really thought of him as Japanese. He looked just like any other old Malay man. White kopiah cap, baggy trousers, a bit of goatee on the chin.

But I did remember a story about some villagers beating him senseless after the war. Pak Arshad was already living as a Malay fisherman by then. He lived and worked amongst the Malays.

A group of Malay and Chinese men, riled by his presence, waited for him to return from his fishing trip. As soon as he docked, they dragged him out of the boat and beat him up. To them, Pak Arshad was still Japanese. He was still everything they hated. Pak Arshad was saved by his fellow fishermen who chased the men away with their oars.

It took some time, but gradually, he was accepted by our community. Decades later, hardly anyone remembered his past as a Japanese conscript. His children went to school with my aunt. It was hard to believe all these wild stories about the war because in 1985, things were so… *normal.*

"That war ruined so many people in more ways than we know," Karno observed.

"I'd like to point out that Mat Indera wasn't Javanese. Rather, his stepmom was Javanese," Suryo stressed.

"He was brought up to be one of us," Karno said. "That was why it became *our problem.* He had his bag of magic spells. It was almost impossible to catch him. So we had to do something to stop him. And we did."

To catch a slippery snake

Our conversation on flying blades, lawless Communists and Malay traitors were interrupted by Aunt Salma, who came over with a fresh supply of tea and savouries. My grandfather's cousins thanked her politely.

"Banana fritters. So delicious," Suryo complimented.

"We grew the bananas ourselves," Aunt Salma beamed. "Here, have this tempeh, too." She pushed a plate of deep-fried tempeh slices towards us.

"Wasn't this what they fed Mat Indera the night they captured him?" Karno muttered as he picked up a slice.

"Yes, indeed," Suryo confirmed. "You heard the story, Ahmad?"

"I heard," my grandfather replied. "A fitting end to the bastard."

"What happened to Mat Indera, grandfather?" I asked, curious to know how the traitor met his sticky end.

My grandfather sipped his tea slowly. He put down the cup and stared ahead, his eyes narrowing as he revisited the distant past. This, he told us, was how the snake called Mat Indera was caught by his own kind.

"It was hard for us to swallow the fact that he was behind the brutal massacre of Kepong Hill. A Malay brought up in a Javanese household. A slap in the face for our people. The worst traitor imaginable. He practised witchcraft, and that made it tricky. He, too, could make himself invisible. When pursued, he concealed himself with a spell. The people giving chase thought they saw a machete flying about. It was him wielding it. They just couldn't see him. For a while, nobody could catch him.

"The British were getting irater. The numbers of policemen killed by ambush, both British and Malay, had risen. Gent, the Governor, discouraged the police from patrolling in armoured vehicles. He thought it would make them complacent. He wanted them to be more aggressive, not hiding behind those vehicles. He was a fool. More policemen died as a result. Without the armoured vehicles, they were exposed to ambushes.

"The policemen and the people were very unhappy with Gent. The British resorted to two strategies.

"Firstly, they relocated the Chinese living in the jungle squatters to new villages. Like Yap Village near your military camp in Kluang. These were people who made the squatters their homes during the war. Some were Min Yuen spooks working for the Communists. But I suspect many were just poor people who fled the Japanese.

"Secondly, they created the Home Guards, or HGs, consisting of Chinese volunteers. Mainly planters, farmers and business people. It wasn't long before the HGs, too, were murdered by the Communists. One HG in Perak, a Chinese farmer, was attacked by several of them whilst he was alone at his post. He got stabbed to death. The poor man had no chance against those bastards. Another in Selangor, who volunteered intelligence to the police, had a hand grenade thrown into his home. He survived but was severely wounded.

"For the British, the turning point was in April 1950. Barely two months after the Kepong Hill massacre, two British police officers – or OSPC as we called them – were ambushed whilst on patrol in

Yong Peng. Just down the road. They were in charge of your town, Kluang. No doubt Mat Indera was one of the masterminds behind these attacks. Who else would know Johore and Malacca like the back of his hand?

"The Yong Peng murders were bad. But as it turned out, not the worst. It was the start of the rainy season. October 1951. The High Commissioner, Sir Henry Gurney, decided to take a breather at Fraser's Hill. It was an hour's drive from the capital city. We weren't sure whether the Communists got lucky or they were tipped off, but Sir Henry did what the subsequent High Commissioner wouldn't do. He told his staff *in advance* of his trip.

"His convoy was a Rolls Royce and a Land Rover of six Malayan policemen. They were coming round the bend, halfway up the hill, when the Communists showered them with bullets. The shots punctured the tyre of the Rolls Royce.

"His driver, a Malay police constable by the name of Muhammad Din, managed to pull it up securely. A bullet hit him. Muhammad Din died on the spot. Five of the six policemen were also killed.

"Accounts varied but some said his wife and his personal secretary were injured. Some said they weren't. We don't know. Sir Henry knew they were compromised. So he did exactly what the Malay policemen at Kepong Hill did: sacrifice himself to protect the others.

"He rolled his wife and his personal secretary to the footwell of the Rolls Royce. He then got out, shut the door, and walked towards the Communists. 'This is the King's Highway!' He repeatedly shouted as he walked toward the side of the road. He wanted to distract the Communists from his wife.

"They shot him dead. Later, his wife crawled out of the car to find the body of her husband riddled with bullets. What a tragedy.

"News of the murder plunged Malaya into despair. Even the High Commissioner wasn't safe from the Communists. By this time, the mood of the masses swung heavily against the Communists. Cracks appeared in the ranks of the party. They lost the labour unions, now they lost the people. We heard that a senior Communist had accused the party of betraying the masses, alienating them with acts of terrorism. Guess what? He was executed.

"When Sir Gerald Templer arrived in 1952, the Communists were already divided. He had no experience of jungle warfare. But he knew that the best people to beat the Communists were the natives.

"Sir Gerald was keen not to put us under military rule. No, the confidence had to be rebuilt. What he needed was intel. So he created a division under the Royal Malayan Police called the Special Branch, or SB. *Mata-mata*. The eyes and ears of the government. They were locals, almost always natives. Sir Gerald made sure the British officers integrated well with the Malayan colleagues.

"He recruited, very controversially, a squad of paramilitary headhunters. These were Iban scouts from Sarawak, Borneo. They were called the Sarawak rangers.

"These headhunters were taught to use rifles by the Malayan Scouts – also known by the British as "the SAS". And by the Yorkshire Light Infantry. Of course, the Ibans had a scary edge: they brought home the heads of the enemies. Soon, their reputation soared. They were feared and admired. They also raised alarm in the British press. Headhunting wasn't in line with the Geneva Convention.

"But the enemies they faced also had no regard for law and human lives. For Sir Gerald, the hearts and minds to be won were those of the Malayans, not the enemies. These rangers later became the Royal Ranger Regiments, second only to the Royal Malay Regiment in power."

"So did they catch Mat Indera?" I probed.

"No. Not for some time. And not by the headhunters," my grandfather replied. "The mastermind behind the Fraser's Hill massacre was Chin Peng, not Mat Indera."

"Chin Peng?"

"Yes. He was a kid when he took over the Malayan Communist Party. His boss, Loi Tak, got found out for being a spook for *both* the British and the Japanese! So the bastard disappeared with the party's funds in 1947. Chin Peng actually got an OBE for his war efforts with Force 136. Could you believe that? He was even at the Victory Parade in London! Maybe he was naive, maybe he was easily conned like Mat Indera. But he, too, got twisted by the war. He went down the slippery slope. Chin Peng could've been a hero. But he chose the murderous path. Perhaps he thought falling into line and taking over from Loi Tak was the right thing to do. He miscalculated. Chin Peng's band of bandits murdered Sir Henry and those policemen."

"Mat Indera was too slippery," Karno explained. "He practised black magic. It was as bad as when we were up against the Japanese. They had their strong magic and human sacrifice."

"Human sacrifice? I thought they were just war belligerents," I said, baffled.

"They had this religion. They believed in the supernatural. They used constant companions, like us. They cut heads. They prayed to many gods."

"You mean the *Shinto* religion," I politely corrected. "Wak, that's not witchcraft. That's animism."

My grandfather, fearing that Karno was losing the plot again – he was never the same since the were-tiger incident in 1945 – pressed on with his story.

"Mat Indera was finally defeated by his own friend. A Javanese from Batu Pahat who, for whatever reason, also joined the Communist Party. His name was Mat Tukyo. We heard that he got caught and was given two choices: collaborate or face the noose. These Communists were godless snakes, so naturally he chose his life over his friend's.

"It was a year after Sir Henry was murdered. The police told Mat Tukyo to trick his friend into dinner.

"Mat Indera accepted his dinner invitation. He came to Mat Tukyo's house with his guard and his adopted son, a 12-year-old boy. Mat Tukyo fed him coffee and fried tempeh laced with purple datura flower. That flower is poisonous, as we'd know. Mat Indera passed out. The SBs quietly finished off his guard outside the house.

"God knows what happened to the boy, if they snuffed him out, too, or if he was given up for adoption. I assume the police were kinder to children than the Communists were to those children on Kepong Hill.

"Because of his practice in witchcraft, they put a spell on him. They tied his arms and legs with straws of long grass. Imagine! Not handcuffs but *long grass*. And that was how they nabbed Mat Indera."

I scratched my chin, puzzled by this fantastical story of traitors, murders and witchcraft. I looked at Adam. He shrugged his shoulders in response.

"Did he get the sticky end he deserved?" I asked.

"No. But we knew better. We let the British deal with him," my grandfather said. "He got sentenced to death by hanging. When was it? Oh yes, 1953. Maybe a more fitting end. No hero's death. Just the coloniser's gallows for him."

"So no more flying daggers after that?" I stupidly asked out of scepticism.

My grandfather looked at my face intently. He was aware I was just a kid who found it hard to believe an old man's story.

"Why don't you ask your mother's family about it?" He suggested.

I was taken aback. We all knew my mother and her family were very much against superstitions.

"Her own grandmother was a bomoh. Her family was big into these things. Not the kongsi side, I'd imagine. Your sinkheh forefathers weren't so keen on Malay witchcraft."

I didn't know what he meant by that, but that remark took me by surprise. I knew one side of my mother's maternal line were people that came by boat two centuries ago. But I had no knowledge about the kongsi bit. Isn't that supposed to be a dodgy secret society?

Also, I had no idea her own grandmother was a bomoh. A bomoh is a witch. Her family was so religious. This would have been against their faith. My grandfather chuckled: "Those men probably didn't know what they were marrying into."

Wednesday, 20 February 1985

My father thought his uncles' magic and the fuss over the spells were all bullshit.

As soon as he arrived on Wednesday morning, we told him about the Popsicle man. About the incident at the fish pond. About the spells, and of course, the flying blades. He wasn't pleased to hear them.

He was also not pleased to learn that Suryo and Karno were with us. My father didn't think they were a good influence on the young ones. Luckily, both men left the day before my father arrived.

That very afternoon, after lunch, we departed to join our mother and sisters up north. During the three-hour drive, I told my father that Karno revealed he was a Red Sash vigilante. My father shook his head in disapproval.

"Karno was all things he *shouldn't have been*," he said.

The matriarch

Friday, 22 February 1985

I didn't nose around until Friday, two days after we arrived at my mother's family home in Perak. That noon, the men in the family, including my father and Adam, went for Friday prayer. Normally, the men wouldn't come back immediately, especially during the holiday season. They'd take their time hanging out with friends at roadside food stalls or coffee shops. That provided me with the perfect opportunity to ask some questions. I had to make sure I did this whilst my mother was occupied with her mother looking after our great-grandmother.

My great-grandmother, an old lady with a body weakened by age, had a mind as sharp as a knife. My great-grandmother, whom we called "Moyang", was rather scary. I had no idea she was a bomoh, though. Her daughter, my grandmother, whom we called "Opah", was the opposite: quiet, reticent and shy.

Moyang lived in a big, old wooden house just opposite Opah's house. It was all wooden, dark brown in colour. At its height, the house was majestic, ornate and decorated with fine wood carvings. It dated back to the 1890s. The furniture and dinner sets, including the coloured glass decanters, hinted at a glorious past before the war – that of a nobility.

Though she was no longer wealthy and the house was old, Moyang insisted on being served by her children and grandchildren. She insisted on having a serving of betel leaves, betel nuts and slaked lime – carefully placed in a beautiful silver container – on the living room table every day. She was toothless by the time I was born, so I rarely saw her chewing betel leaves. I was told the betel leaves were meant for guests who came to visit. But nobody visited her. Everyone visited Opah instead at the opposite house. So who were they for? I had no idea. None of us knew.

Still, as little children, we loved playing with the kacip, the ornate bronze cutter used to cleave the nuts into fine slices. Moyang didn't mind us playing with it, funnily enough. Our mother wouldn't let us near sharp instruments when we were young. Moyang, however, just watched us silently as we cleaved the nuts happily. Her eyes were attentive and inquisitive, and yet she said nothing. She just sat there, a tiny heap of wild white hair and loose, wrinkly skin, studying her great grandchildren and the way they played with a very sharp object.

She was still scary to us kids, though. When we were done playing, we put the kacip back where it belonged in the silver container, bowed to her hastily and ran off to Opah's house.

I was relieved that on Friday, the duty to cook and feed Moyang fell on our mother and Opah. I was beginning to enjoy Madonna's *Lucky Star* on *MTV* on telly when I was interrupted by my aunt, Wan Teh. She was in charge of lunch. She told Hagar, Sarah and I to follow her to the kitchen. She pointed to a big blue plastic bucket on the kitchen table. We peered inside. It was filled with around 20 to 30 small gourami fish, fresh out of water, flipping about and gasping for air. Each was no bigger than my palm. My grandmother had caught them and brought them back from the family's plot of paddy fields.

"I want you to pick up a fish," she instructed. She lifted a gourami out of the bucket. "Be careful of the spiny fins. They can prick you. Then lay it flat like this on the wooden chopping board and—" Wan Teh smashed the poor thing with the flat of her cleaver, "—kill it like this. Then you descale it like so… and toss it to that red bucket. We'll clean them all later. Choose a cleaver, ladies." She gestured towards three cleavers neatly arranged on the kitchen table.

I duly picked one up. "What's for lunch?" I asked.

"Fried gouramis," replied Wan Teh.

"Oh, yummy!" Hagar cried excitedly. She smacked a fish. "This is fun," she said as she descaled it, spreading the silvery scales everywhere.

"Look! I can kill it in seconds!" Maryam shrieked happily as she decapitated a gourami with one chop. The knife was embedded in the chopping board.

"Good precision," I complimented, "But we're supposed to smack it dead like this—" I smashed a gourami dead with the flat of my cleaver, "—not like that, you monkey."

"Hai..yah!" Maryam banged the flat of her cleaver on the head of another gourami. "Like that? Like that?"

"I'm faster," Hagar said. She slapped the flat of her blade on a gourami. The fish's head, flattened, spread like a pressed flower on her chopping board. Its eyeballs popped out.

"Good kill," I praised.

"Girls! Don't play with your food," Wan Teh scolded us. "Just kill the fish."

So we did that for 20 minutes or so. We smacked a gourami dead, we descaled it, and we tossed it into the red bucket. After a while, I carefully probed: "Our Grandpa Syed was a policeman, right, before he became a farmer?" Wan Teh paused. She looked at me. She rarely got asked about her late father, who died six months before I was born, 14 years earlier.

"He was in the Special Branch from 1948 until 1953. And then he quit and moved to this village," Wan Teh said.

"Why did he quit?"

"It was a dangerous time."

Wan Teh put down her cleaver and reflected briefly. Then she resumed her activity of smashing the fish dead for dinner.

"He was originally stationed in his hometown, Parit, up the road," Wan Teh revealed, "But he found it too quiet save one bicycle theft. So he asked to be transferred. You can say he tempted fate. Because not long after he requested it, the State of Emergency was declared."

"Oh. How unfortunate," I said.

"What happened?" Hagar asked.

"The murder spree began," my aunt said. "The Communists pissed off too many people after the war. They were a nuisance. Nobody had time for them. So they did things the hard way to make us suffer. They made a grave mistake when they killed those Englishmen in the plantations."

And this, she said, was how it happened in Kuala Kangsar, a town two hours away from us, on 16 June 1948.

"That night, they killed three British planters. A manager of the Elphil Estate, and the manager of Phin Soon estate and his assistant. I think the Communists killed other people as well. Civilians. Home Guards. The British shut down Kuala Kangsar. Soon after, they shut down the entire country.

"That was the beginning of the State of Emergency. The problem was, the Indian troops had left us after India achieved independence in 1948. So we were left with only a few British troops, a few Gurkha troops and two Royal Malay Regiments. It was really bad.

"Your grandfather, Syed Mokhtar, joined the SB as soon as he turned 18. He was transferred to Kuala Kangsar after the Emergency was declared. Apparently, he enjoyed working with his team. He never told us this, but we read the letters of correspondence he left behind.

"He was part of a five-men team. The leader was an OSPC called Matthew Bruce. He was from some place called Edinburgh. The other two seniors were Sergeant Jacob Abrahamson and Sergeant Lindsey Wright. The other three Malays in the team were, let me recall their names... Meor Hassan, Yeop Ahmad and Uda Ali. Their main job was to supply intelligence to the Malayan Security Force and the British Military Force. Your grandfather was the youngest in the team.

"He was close to Sergeant Wright. It turned out that he, too, like your grandfather, joined the Royal Malayan Police because he wanted something more mundane than his office job in London! He was a banker. From a very good English family. They granted his wish, put him on the ship to Malaya, and promoted him to Sergeant as soon as he got put on the train to Perak!

"Little did he know of the danger of the job. But then, quite a few of the SBs were Chindits of the Burmese campaigns, if not former prisoners of war. They had been through danger and hardship. They could have chosen to return home but they chose to stay.

"Sergeant Abrahamson was a Chindit. Your grandfather asked him why he joined the Royal Malayan Police, after his bitter experience in Burma. He said that if he'd left early, he wouldn't get to see his job finished in Malaya. 'What job is that?' Your grandfather asked. 'To get the people to the other side,' he said, 'Make sure they have the country they deserve.'

"Sergeant Wright, a newbie, really enjoyed being shown around by his mata-mata. Being here lifted his spirit. He told your grandfather the mood in the UK was dark after the war. There was a lot of sadness. He needed some sunshine. Some happiness. Poor man. He didn't get to enjoy that for long.

"One night, Meor didn't return to his post from his usual round. Worried, the men set out to look for him. Your grandfather found Meor dead, slumped outside a shop. I think that spooked your grandfather. All Meors are related to our clan, so he was very upset.

"Months later, Yeop, the most experienced of the mata-mata, was found slumped over a table in a roadside stall, a bullet in his head. And it wasn't even the end of 1950.

"The following year, in 1951, they lost their mentors. One afternoon, OSPC Bruce and Sergeant Abrahamson were called to a village near Tanjung Malim to investigate the disruption to the water supply. It was suspected sabotage.

"Sergeant Wright had a bad feeling about it. He insisted on following them. They refused. They said they'd travel in daylight and return early before sundown. On the way there, in broad daylight, they got ambushed by the Communists and were killed.

"Sergeant Wright had the sad honour of picking up the bodies of OSPC Bruce and Sergeant Abrahamson from the murder scene. He didn't talk about it much. He didn't cry like the others did. But from the letters that we read, he got himself really, really drunk just to forget. It took him some time before he shook it off and sobered up. Everyone knew he was very sad."

At this point, we were done with the fish. Wan Teh lifted the red bucket of descaled fish and walked toward the kitchen sink. Hagar and Sarah mopped the table top whilst I swept the floor.

"The turning point for your grandfather was when the Communists kidnapped his cousin. Your great-grandmother's youngest brother," Wan Teh said.

"Moyang's youngest brother?" I pondered. "She had two brothers."

"Three," Wan Teh corrected. "There were three." She placed the bucket into the sink and turned around to face us. "Your great-grandmother rarely talked about him. But she had a little brother. The Communists murdered him. They did that to get back at your grandfather. Because he was a Special Branch policeman."

The night of the flying blades

My mother descended from an old family in Perak. Its line stretched back hundreds of years to a semi-mythical progenitor, Merong Mahawangsa – part man, part deity, part legend. There was a book written about him. A very ancient book.

For us, the faceless descendants, we mattered little to history. Those that piled over the throne – namely our distant cousins – did their best to park their bums on that royal seat. Whilst they jostled for position, we, the common cousins, did our best to survive the onslaughts of invasions that hit us century after century.

There was a touch of indigenous in our bloodline, of Semang and Batak extractions. A millennia of assimilation saw the family absorbing outsiders at different points of time. Renegades from fallen Malay kingdoms. Princely Siamese outcasts. Central Asian and Arab merchants escaping persecutions in the 16th Century. Indians from the Brahman Buddhist time. Indians from the Victorian time. Sinkheh from Southern China who fled famine and an opium-ravaged kingdom for a better life. These were my kinsmen.

World War 2, understandably, had been hard on my mother's family. As expected, they put up a fight. Lives were lost. The suffering, however, didn't disappear with the retreat of the Japanese. Far from it. The Communists – godless people that they were – wanted no peace but every piece of our land. They were willing to kill our children for it.

One such child was my great-grandmother's youngest brother. He was also the cousin of my late grandfather. This was the story of Syed Hussain, as told by my aunt.

"Syed Hussain was 14, the son of our grandfather's second wife. He was sent to live with Moyang – his older half-sister – after the war. Parit was deemed safer than Kuala Kangsar during the Emergency period. He attended the local school with your great-grandmother's children.

"Syed Hussain was more like a son than a brother to her. Outside school, he looked after their cows and goats. He was obedient and hard-working. His body was slight. Thin arms, thin legs, a small tum. He didn't eat much whilst he was growing up. The war had been hard on him as a child. When people couldn't afford rice, they ate tapioca. Fried grasshoppers were a staple. If they had rice, the seasoning would be salt. That was it. Syed Hussain looked fragile but he was no burden to anyone. The family loved him.

"One Sunday morning, the boy left with a cow for the riverbank. He wanted to give it water and a wash. Before he left, Moyang told Syed Hussain to return early. She and her husband had a rich catch of gourami fish from the paddy fields. They were going to have fried gouramis for lunch. 'Save me some,' the boy said excitedly, as he towed the cow towards the river.

"He didn't return by noon. By 3 pm, the villagers beat the drums at the mosques in the area, signalling an emergency. The boy had gone missing. Before the evening prayer, the villagers found the cow dead by the river. It was slashed to death. Your great-grandmother feared the worst.

"Your grandfather rushed back from Kuala Kangsar on Monday as soon as he heard. Syed Hussain was his first cousin, after all. He was given leave by Sergeant Wright. They looked for him in the river, by the river, in the plantations and they found nothing. Just the dead cow.

"The following day, a few men from the search party arrived at Moyang's place with the grim news. They found the boy. Despite objections from the men and her husband, your Moyang insisted on visiting the murder spot. 'Take me to him,' she said as she covered her hair with a shawl. They took her to a secluded spot half a mile away from the riverbank.

"There, she saw him, her little brother, tied to a banyan tree, his body flopping to one side. Cuts made by blades criss-crossed the thin little body. Blood, by then congealed and blackened, streaked down his sides. The bastards tortured him whilst he was alive. She stepped forward to inspect his face. He looked asleep. The deep, gaping wounds on his neck, however, spoke of the horror done to the boy. He was slaughtered like an animal.

"Your Moyang stuffed her cotton shawl into her mouth. She doubled over. And she screamed. Her crying went on for some time. It was a mixture of anger, sorrow and grief. Her husband didn't dare to touch her. It took a while before she regained herself. She then took a small knife out and began to untie Syed Hussain. The men stepped forward to help. They brought the body home, everyone solemn and silent on the way back.

"Our clan mourned Syed Hussain for the next 40 days. We were told your Moyang hardly uttered a word during the mourning period. She didn't cry much towards the end of it. By then, it was obvious why the boy was singled out by the Communists. In our clan, there was a person that worked as a mata-mata for the defence forces. Your grandfather Syed Mokhtar. It was revenge.

"Our clan waited until after Ramadhan, the holy month, to make their move. It was the end of June 1952. During the Syawal celebration of Aidilfitri, a few men of the clan visited their Banjarese neighbours who lived at Gajah Village, 40 km away upriver.

"They were children of the Banjarese settlers who came from Banjarmasin, south of Borneo, before the war. They were descendants of the Dayak headhunters who converted to Islam and became Malay. Like the Javanese, they kept to themselves. But also like the Javanese, they got hassled by men of their own tribe who extorted 'protection fee' on behalf of the Malayan Communist Party.

"Fired up by the Indonesian War of Independence against the Dutch, these young Communists of Banjarese and Javanese descent thought we should also topple the British in the same manner after the war. Many didn't subscribe to this view. They migrated to Malaya to avoid revolutions.

"Our clansmen were curious to know how the Banjarese fared after an incident that broke out just before the holy month.

An elder of the village confronted a Banjarese Communist who was extorting money from the villagers. The young Communist punched the elder in the face. 'I'll take you out and blow your brains here if you stop me again,' the thug warned, pointing to the stolen rifle slung over his shoulder.

"Ah, by that time, the rice had overcooked and turned to porridge. The thug had said the unthinkable to the old man. He issued a challenge. *A fatal challenge.* The elder swiftly took out his machete – a parang bungkol optimised for cutting long grass, as well as human heads – and cut off the ruffian's hands and legs.

"It was gruesome but it didn't shock the villagers. The Banjarese are descendants of the fearsome Dayaks after all. The warrior's blood runs thick in their veins.

"Barely alive, the Communist was left by the riverside by his own tribe for his comrades to discover. It was a stern warning: enemies would be killed, but traitors of the race were certainly not tolerated. The severest punishment was reserved for them.

"His comrades found his dead body days later, when they dared to sneak out to the site. They were enraged. They vowed revenge on the Banjarese settlers. So they set upon the hut of a Malay family – not related to the Banjarese tribe – and burned it down.

"Because the Communists taking part were Chinese, the situation escalated into a racial tension. It was a mess. The kind of evil that this type of situation generates. Communities that had been living peacefully with each other along that stretch of river for generations were now on high alert.

"The Banjarese settlers were asked by our clansmen if they would help us get rid of the Communists, once and for all. Our men told them what happened to Syed Hussain. They said yes.

"The newly formed alliance sent a warning to the Communists to retreat from the Perak riverside by Thursday night, 10 July 1952. If they were still around on that night, the Red Sash would come for them.

"The Communists were spooked. Borrowing from the British's divide-and-conquer strategy, the Communists then spread rumours to the Chinese in the area that the Malays – lackeys of the Japanese – were going to kill them. Some believed the rumour and pledged support. Some got their arms twisted to support the Communists against their will. Many simply packed up and left for towns downriver to avoid trouble. A few went back into the jungle to hide, as they did during the Japanese occupation. For these unfortunate people, the cycle of suffering continued.

"Your grandfather was kept out of the loop of this unfolding situation because he was an SB. He only found out when, at the end of Syawal, during a visit to your Moyang's place, he chanced upon two of his male cousins filling up water in the huge stoneware jars at the back of the house.

'What's that for?' He questioned.

'Garangsang water,' a cousin replied, before he was hushed by the other. Your grandfather's suspicion was roused.

'Magic water? Why in so many jars?'

'Uh. It's ablution water for Friday prayer. For the mosque.'

'Garangsang water for *Friday prayer*?'

"As he scanned the jars, he realised something was wrong. You don't need magic water or holy water for the Friday congregation. The water was meant not just for any congregation. Most likely intended for an army of men. Or women. Garangsang water, when drunk, turns one into a ferocious fighter who lusts for blood. In fact, before we were Muslims, that was what we used the tempayan for. To brew tapai, tuak or to concoct garangsang water, amongst other things. Your grandfather turned to inspect his cousins. Both wore black clothes.

'Show me your red sash,' he demanded.

"They hesitated. Then they produced their red sashes from the pockets of their trousers.

'Where's this face-off going to be? And when?' Your grandfather asked. Cornered, they told him everything.

"Although conflicted, your grandfather confided in Sergeant Wright. He was worried Sergeant Wright would deem his report too fantastical. To his relief, his superior listened attentively. Admittedly, after Sir Henry Gurney's assassination the year before, the policy of 'shout first, shoot later' was withdrawn. If vigilantes mobilised against the Communists, the police could well turn a blind eye. But the law is the law.

'We have to stop them,' Sergeant Wright advised. 'Also, you wouldn't want your family to be accomplices.'

'No,' your grandfather concurred.

"Two teams were formed to mobilise that very night of July 1952. The first team consisted of five Royal Malayan policemen. The second team consisted of another five – Sergeant Wright and your grandfather amongst them.

"The first team went to investigate the local mosque at our village just as the dusk prayer began. They arrived to find some 30 men sitting on the floor chanting 'There is no god but God', their bodies swaying from side to side in a trance. The police didn't find this unusual. The men hadn't left the mosque, so all was fine.

"The police then checked the women's section of the mosque. There, they found about 20 women chanting as well. Your Moyang was one of them. She was seated in the first saf – the first row – with the more elderly women. Only one of the women – a young girl – turned around to look at the policemen as they drew the curtain to peer inside. That was your grandmother.

"The rest simply focussed on their chanting. Their bodies in white, long prayer garments swayed gently from side to side. The movement was so gentle it looked like the women would float and fly away at any time. Like angels. Their voices, higher pitched, combined with the baritone of male voices, had a mesmerising effect.

"The policemen concluded nothing was amiss. They radioed Sergeant Wright, who was with the other team, to tell them they found nothing out of order.

"Sergeant Wright pressed for more information:
'What are they doing?'
'Chanting. About 30 men and 20 women.'
'Have you checked the stoneware jars?'
'Yes.'
'And?'
'Empty.'

"With this information, that second team took their Land Rover to Gajah Village. They stopped by a rubber estate. It was pitch dark, around 9 pm. There was no light except for the stars in the sky and the moon, partly obscured behind a curtain of clouds.

"The first sound they picked up was that of the crickets and nocturnal animals. Slowly, the policemen worked out sounds similar to balloons being popped. They were faint. They were gunshots. It came from a jungle area at the edge of the plantation, towards the river. The policemen advanced carefully and slowly towards the noise. When they reached the edge, Sergeant Wright signalled the three colleagues to stay behind. He beckoned your grandfather to follow him. They slipped into the darkness, swallowed by monstrous trees, tall grass and the cacophonic sound of crickets and rattling guns.

"They emerged on the other side to witness a bloodbath, a scene of confusion and unimaginable horror.

"On the river, a moored boat sat idle. It was barely visible because of the thick fog surrounding it. They found it strange because it was a warm July night.

"On the foreshore of the river, about 30 or so Communist guerrillas shot wildly and aimlessly at the night sky. They looked mad and terrified. Several screamed and then fell to the ground, limbs and heads detaching from their bodies. It looked like they were trying to get to the boat. They were trying to escape.

"Sergeant Wright blinked back in disbelief. Rain drops began to fall, or so he thought. He wiped the wetness off his face, looked down to his hand and realised they weren't raindrops. They were sprays of blood.

"It took some time before Sergeant Wright could make out the glistening steels soaring and zigzagging in the air. His nose picked up the most disturbing scent, the smell of blood mingled with steel.

"He looked at your grandfather, terrified. Your grandfather's face had turned as white as a sheet. It finally dawned on your grandfather that there was no Red Sash army. They weren't there. An invisible 'army' was sent to wield the weapons on their behalf. The garangsang water wasn't for humans.

"In the confusion, Sergeant Wright heard a click. He abruptly turned towards the sound. A Communist had caught Sergeant Wright in his cross hairs. Sergeant Wright stared down the barrel of the rifle, frozen in fear. This is the end, he thought. 'You fucking Englishman,' the Communist muttered in Malay, 'I'll send you back to your fucking hell.'

"The Communist pulled the trigger. It was jammed. He pulled again. Nothing happened. Baffled, he looked down to check his rifle. Like lightning, a machete zipped past. The Communist crumpled down. His head rolled to one side. The eyes in the head rolled erratically and blinked rapidly as life ebbed away.

"Sergeant Wright could barely register the scene

before he was distracted by the scream of another Communist. A spear went deep into his stomach. It wriggled itself out, eliciting screams from the victim. It finally came out, pulling the man's intestines out. It then flew away on its own. Sergeant Wright felt a tug on his sleeve. It was your grandfather. 'Let's get out of here,' he whispered.

"Both men ran towards their position at the plantation. They were stopped in their tracks by another Communist. His rifle pointed squarely at your grandfather's head. The bastard was ready to blast his face off. He hunched down as he squeezed the trigger. That, too, was jammed. A small keris, its blade no longer than the size of a man's hand, swooped out of the darkness and slashed his exposed neck.

"Shocked, the Communist dropped his rifle and covered the wound with his hand. The flying keris made a U-turn and repeatedly stabbed the man in the chest and stomach. Each penetration was followed by twisting and wrenching movements, making the wounds bigger. Blood spouted forth. In a matter of minutes, the man collapsed to the ground, lifeless.

"The keris swung around and charged towards Sergeant Wright. 'Stop! I know who your master is!' Your grandfather cried, his outstretched hands trembling.

"He recognised the wavy shape and the unusual shallow grooves of thumbprints on the sides of the blade. The keris froze, suspended mid-air, the sharp end pointing threateningly at Sergeant Wright.

'Datuk, jangan bunuh sahabat saya!'
Sir, don't kill my friend.
'Saya tahu asal-usulmu!'
I know your origin.
"Your grandfather cited the name of his father, his grandfather and his clan, and the kings before him —

before the time of the Larut Wars, before the time of the Malaccan Sultans, before the time of the Fanged King and before the time of Gangga Negara. As he did so, the keris slowly circled around Sergeant Wright. It wasn't working.

"Your grandfather pleaded, beseeched, even scolded the blade to submit to him. And then, out of the blue, he cited the name of your great-grandmother. The keris, without warning, bolted off like a shot in the opposite way into the darkness. Your grandfather began to run after it but changed his mind. It wasn't the time and the place. 'Let's leave!' He said to Sergeant Wright. They ran as fast their legs could take them, not looking back.

"It took the policemen a while to clean up the mess by the riverbank. In fact, they had to do it the next day, after radioing the Yorkshire Light Infantry and their Iban trackers, as well as the 1st Manchester Regiment. The policemen didn't want to do it alone.

"An officer from the 1st Royal Malay Regiment also arrived at the scene. He was aghast. He didn't expect to see heads and limbs everywhere. Things like this were in breach of the Geneva Convention. He sternly advised the soldiers and police against taking away heads and hands as evidence – or souvenirs. Sergeant Wright explained to him that none of the defence forces were involved. It was the vigilante. The officer had his doubts but he didn't press further.

"The communities along the River Perak saw dozens of Land Rovers carting out the bodies from the scene. They heard about the decapitations and mutilations. But they had scant knowledge of what really happened on that Thursday night. They later assumed that the military regiments were behind the beheading. None of the regiments denied it though not one owned up to it. They divulged nothing."

And that was the story of my grandfather and his poor cousin. Not long after, my grandfather proposed to my grandmother, his own cousin, and also the daughter of our Moyang. He was a good-looking man. He could have picked any lady from a good, noble family. However, he decided to go for my quiet and plain-looking grandmother. Was it guilt or love? Who knows.

The wedding lifted the family out of the sadness that had plagued them since the war, and those tragic events. Sergeant Wright and colleagues, both British and natives, attended the wedding. They all dressed up in traditional Malay clothes. I saw a picture of them on that wedding day, seated in two rows of chairs, looking very handsome and happy.

I was told that just before 1957, Sergeant Wright returned to the United Kingdom. He quit the police. He didn't go back to his banking job either. He moved to the countryside to manage his family's properties. He wanted to look after his family farm. I truly hope Lindsey Wright found happiness there.

Wan Teh told us that our clan took religion seriously after that incident. They repented. They let go of many "family inheritance". My great-grandmother gave up being a bomoh. She traded spells and charms with prayers and acts of charity. She covered her hair.

As far as I knew, we had no keris or anything like that in the possession of my mother's family. My great-grandmother's heirloom, a small keris that was owned only by the women in the family, was eventually passed on to a female relative. As of 1985, the whereabouts of it was unknown.

When his first son, my uncle Syed Alwi, was old enough to enlist, my grandfather advised him to join the Royal Ranger

Regiment. It originated from the Iban trackers' squad trained by the Malayan Scouts and the Yorkshire Light Infantry. My great-grandmother gave her full blessing. From the 1970s until 1987, my mother's brother and my father fought against the Communists. It was, you can say, a long cycle of retributions and counter-retributions.

Saturday, 23 February 1985

Two days before our holiday ended, the family travelled back to Kluang, to our military camp. In the car, I let slip about Karno and Suryo being with us in Malacca. I also told my mother about Karno being a Red Sash. She wasn't impressed.

"That superstitious lot. When are they going to get with the times?" My mother sighed in despair. She cautioned: "Vigilantes aren't on the right side of the law. You can't take matters into your own hands. So don't listen to too many stories on the Red Sash."

"What about the flying blades that killed the Communists near your village?" I naively asked.

"What flying blades?" My mother responded, genuinely surprised.

"Just some fancy stories about the Emergency era," Adam swiftly interjected, wanting to put an end to the topic. We had two more hours to go before we reached Kluang.

"You don't take those tales seriously," my mother said dismissively. "Many people were depressed after the war. Times were hard. They told tales and fantastic stories to make themselves feel better. The truth was much harder to stomach. Fantasy is the easy way out. Children, there's no such thing as flying blades. Or ghosts."

What my mother really meant was that there is no place for

such things in our modern life. What science can't explain doesn't exist. They only take us backwards, into the past, where horrible history, mistakes, tragedies and dead people belong. We don't look back on those sad days. There is no need.

The dare

There were no more talks of flying blades. Over time, the stories and events faded from our memories. More recent and irresistible events – MTV, Grammy Awards, Malaysian-made cars, government-funded soap operas, private TV channels, New Romantics and English rock bands – occupied our consciousness.

Much later, flying blades and, sadly, even the acts of heroism by the locals and the defence forces – were dismissed as myths. Or consigned to the pages of history, for the consumption of those who bothered to read books. Might as well. In the race to keep up with the other Tiger economies, we left behind history and dogmas that no longer serve our ambition.

There was also no more talk of the Popsicle man and the culprit behind the spells. We only found out about the possible suspect many years later, but by that time, Adam was gravely ill. I put the matter to one side to focus on my ailing brother. I took one thing at a time.

By May 1985, we hadn't heard about the hysteria that afflicted the female recruit of the Volunteer Corps for four months.

And then one day, we had an update. My father, with the help of his batman, Nik, figured out what happened. A week before the incident happened, the volunteers were assigned – as part of their training – sentry duty and night rounds in areas such as Yap Village. One of the rounds covered a Chinese cemetery. It was adjacent to the Buddhist temple. The very temple the female volunteers visited and had their photo shoot at before the hysteria happened.

As a dare, a few of the volunteers on night duty peeled off the ceramic photos of the dead that were mounted on the gravestones in the cemetery. This was done in the middle of the night. It was macabre, not to mention foolish, but these were things people did for fun at the expense of others.

Of course, the instructors knew nothing about this until my father's investigation concluded. The prank stopped abruptly.

After reprimanding those who participated in this activity, my father consulted the army's religious officer about this matter.

The officer responded: "We have to respect others and observe the boundaries. We believe in God but God's creatures are vast and many. The recruits have certainly offended one of them. It's only fair to show our respect."

He then recited a passage from the holy book: "I do not worship what you worship. Nor are you worshippers of what I worship. Nor will I be a worshipper of what you worship. Nor will you be worshippers of what I worship. For you is your religion, and for me is my religion."

"So what do you suggest, ustaz?" My father asked.

"To begin with, they should apologise to the monks at the Buddhist temples."

And that was what the volunteers did. Two representatives went to the temple to meet with the chief monk. They confessed about what had happened. He was surprised. He expressed his concern over the well-being of the lady implicated. The monk wasn't aware that the volunteers were taking photos of the temple without permission. They could have asked, he said. He wouldn't mind at all. But to the monk, this happened in the past.

They asked for his forgiveness, so he forgave them. Before they left, he gave them a blessing, and wished them happiness and enlightenment. He told the volunteers they were welcome to visit again. The temple was open to all. After that, we heard no more stories of supernatural possessions.

The female kesatriya

It was weird that one day, our history teacher mentioned the flying blades as we went through a chapter on the "Darurat" – the Malayan Emergency period. She mentioned the Red Sash vigilante. It was the end of 1985, and we were still in the Emergency period. It was a history lesson. We were only supposed to learn facts. Why were the flying blades mentioned as if they really happened?

"The Communists terrorised us after the war. So the villagers in Muar mobilised and formed the Red Sash," she said, adding an anecdote that certainly didn't appear anywhere in our history book. The Red Sash didn't exist in our history syllabus, despite the fact that many of us knew of its existence. "Yes, we heard stories of flying machetes. That was a scary time."

I remember looking at my history teacher, thinking: 'But my mother told me it was all untrue.' I didn't say anything. None of the students said anything. Rote learning means that Malaysian students aren't encouraged to criticise. They just need to memorise facts. To pass the exam, you only need to repeat what the textbook says.

Of course, along with the Red Sash, Sir Gerald Templer and the Malayan defence forces were erased from our history lessons. Mat Indera, an embarrassment to the Malay and Javanese races, was cut out completely. Chin Peng became a caricature of evil. What he did was truly evil but we all knew that just like Mat Indera, World War Two tripped people over to go down the wrong path. Having witnessed the worst of humanity, they, too, lost their own humanity. God knows how their lives would turn out if the war didn't happen at all. The

Kepong Hill massacre wouldn't have happened. Sir Henry Gurney wouldn't have died. The constant companions wouldn't have been in our lives.

Years later, in London, I spotted a keris with parrot hilt, made of ivory, in the Southeast Asia section of the V&A Museum in South Kensington. It was estimated to be 200 to 300 years old. It was from Perak, believe it or not. Before it was passed on to R.J. Wilkinson, the Deputy Governor of the Straits Settlement from 1911 to 1916, it belonged to one Sultan Idris. I suspect he was the king that ruled sometime after the Larut Wars ended in the late 1870s.

Wilkinson first loaned it to the museum. This, and some other Malayan artefacts, were later bequeathed to the V&A in 1950 after his widow died. The odd thing that jumped out to me was the description card of this display. It mentioned something about the alleged ability of a keris to fly:

"This keris is the distinctive weapon of Malaysia and Indonesia. Some were credited with supernatural powers — the ability to kill merely being pointed at the victim, for example, or to fly through the air to attack an enemy."

I did a double take. I read the description card again and again. I thought: 'Why is this mentioned on a description card at *the V&A Museum in London*? These are items collected and curated by social scientists. The flying keris is meant to be superstition.'

Perplexed and disturbed, I read papers and books by Wilkinson and his higher education officer, R.O. Winstedt. In chapters devoted to shamanism, the flying keris crops up.

In one of his books, Winstedt wrote about female bomohs of royal lineage who heal nobilities by putting them in a trance. He described one who performed the ritual for a king, accompanied by a group of female musicians who played the drums. All of the women 'dressed as men'. I didn't think he was describing cross-dressing women. Rather, Winstedt was describing the serikandi attire — the female warrior attire that originated from our time as Brahman Buddhists.

Females from the kesatriya class who served the military

were known as serikandi. That reminded me of Wan Teh's story of the night of the flying blades. The women involved, including my great-grandmother, weren't just any ordinary women. I recalled the fine furniture and the expensive decanters at Moyang's home – and yes, the betel leaves and nuts in the silver container, forever on offer to some mysterious visitors whom we never saw.

That Thursday night on 10 July 1952, the policemen visited the mosque with the intention to raid and apprehend suspects. They assumed that it was the men who would lead the vigilante assault. This was, of course, proven to be not the case. Because there was *no man* involved. But they did mention to Sergeant Wright that there were 20 or so women – Moyang and my own grandmother amongst them – found chanting in the female section. And they thought nothing of it.

Of course they thought nothing of it. Who would suspect a group of village women – farmers, wives and mothers – doing anything unusual?

Did my grandfather recognise the family heirloom that night? The flying keris? The thumbprints on the sides of the blade weren't only distinctive. They were unusual. It means the ancient blade was flattened not by a hammer but by pressing the red, hot steel with human fingers. This is true with a keris type that antique weapon collectors called 'keris picit' – a keris with a blade that's pressed with thumbs. Whoever makes the keris like this can no doubt withstand the heat. Or he's just plain crazy and loses his digits afterwards.

It was clear to me that my grandfather Syed Mokhtar knew all along. Sergeant Wright also knew. The officer from the Royal Malay Regiment suspected it. My grandfather Raden Ahmad knew. His cousins knew. But my parents and their generation colluded to not let us know. Maybe they didn't know, or didn't want to know. What you can't see, you don't think about.

I recalled the day my great-grandmother died. I was seventeen. I saw her lying peacefully in her bed. Her face was covered with a transparent silk shawl. The rest of her fragile body was covered in batik cloth. My mother wept. My aunt and my uncle wept.

I remember my youngest sister, Maryam, helping herself to the betel leaves and nuts that day. She sat alone at the table in the living room and chewed the folded betel leaf quietly as female relatives paid their last respect to Moyang in her bedroom. I thought it was just her way of dealing with death in the family as a kid. I thought nothing of it then.

But after I read materials by Wilkinson and Winstedt, I found this memory a bit disturbing.

Was Maryam really alone at the table? Were the unseen visitors there? Did they come to pay a visit when Moyang died?

Wan Teh had told me that the keris was later passed on to a female relative. Who? It could be a cousin. It could be my sisters. It could be any of us.

It took a long while for me to accept it but when I finally did, my heart sank in despair. I knew then that the prospect of our constant companion – the unruly servant – being a very distant probability was worsening. The prospect of this monster being very much a part of our life was improving by the day.

GLOSSARY

Banjarese: An ethnic group that originated from the Banjar regions of Kalimantan, Borneo, Indonesia. They were descendants of the Dayak tribe of Borneo, known for their prowess in jungle warfare and their ancient culture of headhunting. The term Banjar was initially used to refer to Javanised Dayak people. Later, especially in Malaysia, it's used to refer to Malaynised people of this ethnicity. Like the Javanese, they're very much integrated into the fabric of Malay communities in Malaysia. The majority of Banjarese people in Malaysia reside in the state of Perak.

Bomoh: A Malay shaman. *Bomoh* is a northern term influenced by Thai language. In southern Malay regions, the term is *pawang* or *dukun*. They perform rituals to heal but they can also do this for wicked spells and curses. Adherents to Islam use Quranic verses and processes deemed not against the faith. Adherents to Buddhism, meanwhile, use their prayers, chants, spells and charms (*tangka*) for their end.

Brahman Buddhism: A form of Buddhism prevalent in Southeast Asia before the arrival of Islam in the Malay Archipelago.

Cirebon, Java: A northern city on the west coast of Java in Indonesia. "Cirebon" means "mixed", a reference to the city's rich amalgamation of Sundanese, Javanese, Arab and Chinese influences.

Constant companion: In some Eastern beliefs, a *qareen* is a constant companion or a double assigned to every human born. It's assumed to be the supernatural part of the human or a ghostly entity that shadows the human's every move. There's a parallel between a *qareen* and a demon in the deified Eastern sense (not the devil), or between deities or demi-gods in the European Antiquity sense. Depending on beliefs, it can be a devilish function or subservient to God and humans. In Malay culture, a constant companion can also be a *saka* – derived from the word *pusaka* meaning inheritance or heirloom – that's passed down for generations, by choice or by default.

Flying blades: A form of Malay magic that sees weapons such as keris, machete, knife and spear being mobilised against the enemies – without any human carrying it. In other words, they fly on their own. Allegedly, anthropologists had witnessed this, or had heard first accounts of this phenomenon. It has been said that it's a magic that makes the assailant carrying the weapon invisible to the eyes of the enemy. The flying blade myth co-exists with the legend woven around the mysterious Red Sash vigilante mobs. The type of machete allegedly used by the Banjarese for this end was the *parang bungkol.*

Garangsang water: A form of water magic in which a spell is cast on plain water that's contained in a *tempayan* or earthenware stone jars. This magic isn't exclusive to the Banjarese people. The Malays call this type of water *air jampi* (water that has a mantra recited over it). Garangsang water has been cited in many blogs as the drink consumed by mobs of vigilantes before they went on a murderous rampage. It's said to rouse a person to be a lethal, blood lusting warrior.

The Fanged King: Also known as *Raja Bersiong.* A descendant of Merong Mahawangsa, King Ong Maha Perita Deria once ruled Langkasuka, now known as the state of Kedah. A palace cook, in her haste, cut her finger whilst preparing spinach for the king's meal. She had it served to the king, anyway. The king, loving the taste of human blood, turned to human sacrifice and feasted on his victims' blood. He was later ousted and his infant son elevated to the throne to become the new king. One of the Fanged King's kinsmen was King Ganji Sarjuna, the founder of Gangga Negara (100 CE-1000 CE), a district under the state of Perak.

Geneva Convention: Article 15, first paragraph of the 1949 Geneva Convention I states that parties to the conflict must take all possible measures to prevent the dead from being despoiled. The UK Military Manual (1958) also insists that "the dead must be protected against pillage", specifying that "this is a well-established rule of customary international law". Malaysia's Armed Forces Act (1972) provides that "every person subject to service law under this Act" who steals or plans to steal from the person killed in "warlike operations" can be convicted by court-martial to imprisonment.

Hat Yai Treaty: The Hat Yai Treaty in 1989 marked the end of the 21-year Communist insurgency in Malaysia. It was signed and ratified by the Malayan Communist Party (MCP), and the Malaysian and Thailand governments in Hat Yai, 48 km from the Malaysian border, on 2 December 1989. Some 1200 guerrillas laid down their arms and returned to civilian life. A 41-year-old curfew was lifted across Malaysia in response.

Headhunting: A war ritual in Borneo up to the 1960s, and once upon a time, widespread throughout Southeast Asia, in which the enemies' heads were cut off as tokens. They were used in spiritual ceremonies, displayed during harvest festivals and treated like supernatural protectors of those who keep them. During harvest festivals, the skulls are taken out for display and can be seen hung from the ceiling, bunched together with paddy stalks and other decorations.

Home Guard: During the Emergency period, whilst Malays were recruited for the Royal Malay Regiment and the Royal Malayan Police, Chinese volunteers who were farmers, planters and businessmen were recruited as Home Guard volunteers. They contributed greatly to the safety of the communities, putting their lives at risk in doing so. The Home Guards formed the basis of the Malaysia Volunteers Corp Department, or RELA.

Keris: A dagger with a distinctive wavy blade. Originated from Java but is prevalent throughout the Malay Archipelago and parts of Indochina – particularly in former Champa kingdoms – as a symbol of strength and indomitable spirit. It's also believed to possess supernatural powers. R J Wilkinson, the Deputy Governor of the Straits Settlement from 1911 to 1916, in his description for a display at the V&A Museum in London, UK, states that the keris can fly ('flying dagger'). "This kris is the distinctive weapon of Malaysia and Indonesia. Some were credited with supernatural powers – the ability to kill merely being pointed at the victim, for example, or to fly through the air to attack an enemy." Owners of 'supernatural' daggers smoke theirs with incense and bathe the blade in lime juice as a form of offering. See 'flying blades'.

Kongsi: Hokkien term for "company". In the 1800s, at the height of the Larut Wars, kongsi was associated with underground Chinese syndicates that arranged the migration of *sinkhehs* (indentured labourers from Southern China), legal or otherwise, as well as groups committed to banditry during those conflicts. The truth is far more complicated, as kongsi members then weren't necessarily criminals but merely migrants who paid extortionate fees to work in Malaya. Today, the term is used to indicate an association that a Chinese clan belongs to. In the Malay language, it also means "to share". The modern term *kongsi gelap* (dark kongsi) can refer to triads of Chinese, Malay or Indian ethnicity.

Kuala Kangsar, Perak: A royal town of Perak, a northern state in Malaysia. Up to 1875, royal towns were strategically located mainly in Beruas, a maritime district, often on high grounds and in well-protected capes or estuaries. Under British rule, after the assassination of Perak's first British Resident J.W.W Birch in 1875, Kuala Kangsar – a very exposed riverside settlement – was made a royal town instead.

Malayan Anti-Japanese People's Army (MPAJA): A paramilitary group that resisted the Japanese occupation from 1941 to 1945. The MPAJA was a collaboration between the Malayan Communist Party (MCP) and the British Force 136 special operations team. In the 14 days between the surrender of Japan and the British Military Administration takeover, MCP reprisals such as kangaroo court trials of Japanese soldiers and their collaborators led to unlawful executions. Some, unfortunately, were mistakenly carried out against innocent civilians. This brief period of chaos undermined the MPAJA's war efforts. The group was disbanded in December 1945.

Malayan Emergency: A guerrilla war fought in British Malaya between the military forces of the British Empire and Commonwealth, and the Malayan Communist Party (MCP). It began in 1948 and carried on until 1960, three years after Peninsular Malaysia gained independence from the British. The insurgency continued against Malaysia until 1989.

Mata-mata: See 'The Royal Malayan Police'.

Merlimau, Malacca: A town in the Jasin district of Malacca in Peninsular Malaysia, some 22 km away from the ancient city of Malacca, and about 230 km from Singapore.

Moyang: Malay for "great-grandmother".

Parang bungkol: A type of long machete used by the Banjarese people.

Peninsular Malaysia: The Malaysian part of the Malay Peninsula. The Malay Peninsula covered the entirety of West Malaysia and the south of Thailand. States in these areas in both countries were once united under several kingdoms throughout the centuries.

River Muar: A river that flows via three states, Negeri Sembilan, Malacca and Johore, in the southern part of Peninsular Malaysia.

Opah: Perakian Malay term for "grandmother".

Pelikat: A sarong for men made of chequered cotton cloth. Before sanitary pads were introduced, Malayan women used old pelikat cloths during menstruation.

The Red Sash: A direct translation of the Malay term *selepang merah*. Selepang is a type of shawl or *kesa* draped diagonally over one's shoulder. Merah means red. This is the name of a group of Malay vigilante groups that formed and reformed several times during Malaya's and Malaysia's tumultuous periods of the State of Emergency and racial conflicts between 1945 and 1969. Originally formed after the war by Javanese communities in Johore to resist the Communists, the concept gained ground elsewhere in Malaya where locals were compelled to mobilise against terrorists. In the 1950s, this group was led by the Banjarese communities in Perak. In 1969, troubles were concentrated only in the capital city and Selangor. It wasn't certain if the Red Sash vigilante group mobilised there. The Red Sash is noted not only for its membership of martial art experts, but also in the use of magic. See 'flying blades'.

The Royal Malay Regiment: Malaysian Army's regiment

comprising the mechanised infantry, light infantry and parachute infantry. It was formed by the British War Office in 1933 at the request of Malay kings a decade before. The primarily land-based regiment replaced the traditional Malay military structure formed by hereditary roles within noble houses that were heavily influenced by thalassocracy (maritime empires).

The Royal Malayan Police: The Federation of Malaya Police began in Penang in 1806. In the 1870s, at the height of the Larut Wars in Perak, the Perak Armed Police was formed. The Federated Malay States Police, formed in 1896, was the body that looked after the states of Perak, Selangor, Negeri Sembilan and Pahang. Under the British system, policemen were recruited from European and Indian backgrounds. Around 1905, Malays were encouraged to join. The federation remained until 1942. The Federation of Malayan Police came to prominence during the Emergency period of 1948 to 1960. The murder of the High Commissioner, Sir Henry Gurney, in 1951, by Communist terrorists led to the appointment of Sir Gerald Templer, a former general of the Royal Irish Fusiliers. Sir Gerald didn't want to impose military rule in order to restore public confidence in Malaya. He introduced an intelligence arm called the Special Branch (SB). The policemen, commonly of Malay ethnicity, were called *mata-mata* (eyes). Sir Gerald masterminded the strategy of "winning the hearts and minds" which proved to be a success, but only in Malaya. The Communists, starved of popular support and public approval, were driven into the jungle.

The Royal Ranger Regiment: An infantry regiment of the Malaysian Army. It originated from the Sarawak Rangers, established in 1862 under the White Rajah, Charles Brooke. Absorbed into the Malaysian Army, the rangers developed a fearsome reputation as fierce warriors, fashioned after their hero, Rentap. Rentap, or Libau son of Ningkan, was an Iban chief who rebelled against the British. His war cry, "Agi idup, agi ngelaban!" ("Whilst I'm alive, I fight!) is the motto of the regiment and the war cry of modern-day rangers.

Saka: See 'constant companion'.

Saudara baru: Literally means 'new brother'. A convert to Islam. The Malays, following the Austro-Polynesian custom, expand this to mean 'to be a new Malay'. Regardless of ethnic background and DNA, a person who becomes *saudara baru* is considered a Malay and will be protected at all costs in times of trouble.

Sinkheh: Possibly Hokkien for "newcomer'. Refers to Southern Chinese migrants, all of them men, who came to Malaya in the 1800s as indentured labourers. They came from the regions of Fujian and Kwantung to escape famine, political instability or persecution. Upon arrival in Malaya, they spent one year as indentured labourers, chained to the snakeheads, before they earned their freedom. Until the 1930s, when the migration of Chinese women into Southeast Asia was finally permitted, sinkhehs and their descendants married local women. Many also married into the Malay communities and became *saudara baru*. Modern politics group them together with the Peranakan Chinese – those who came as courtiers and Ming envoys during the 1500s. Today, the distinction amongst the Hokkiens, the Cantonese and the Hakkas is subtle. When they first arrived two centuries ago, the sinkhehs of Hakka and Cantonese origins were considered separate from the Peranakans. See 'saudara baru'.

Special Branch: See 'The Royal Malayan Police'.

State of Emergency: On 16 June 1948, Communist insurgents murdered three British plantation managers and one Chinese contractor in Perak, and another Chinese person in Johore. In the River Siput murders, Elphil Estate manager A E Walker was shot at his office desk at 8.30 am. Less than an hour later, Phin Soon Estate manager John Allison and his assistant Ian Christian were tied and killed by the Communists. This was about a mile away from the Elphil Estate. The State of Emergency was declared in Perak the following day, and to the entire Malaya soon after. The Indian regiments had left after India's independence in 1948. The regiments left – or called – to protect Malaya from this moment on were:

- RAMD 1 and 2 (1st and 2nd Malay Battalion)
- Special Air Service or SAS Squadron A (Ipoh), Squadron B and C (Johore, supported by Royal Inniskillings)
- King's Own Yorkshire Light Infantry (they trained the Iban trackers to use the rifles)
- 1st and 2nd Battalion, Lincolnshire Regiment; 1st Manchester Regiment (Perak, Perlis and Kedah)
- six Gurkha regiments: 48th Gurkha Brigade, 17th Gurkha Division, 2nd, 6th, 7th and 10th of the Gurkha Rifles, Gurkha Signals, Engineers and Transport Regiments.

The SAS Squadrons were also known as the Malayan Scouts. In February 1951, for Operation Helsby, the parachute troops attacked the communists in the Belum Valley, Perak, on the border of Thailand.

Tapai: Sweet, fermented rice or tapioca. Within indigenous culture where alcohol is still consumed, tapai is the alcoholic brew made from rice or tapioca. The alcoholic version can be called *tuak*, although tuak is also made of fermented coconut nectar.

Tempayan: The earthenware stone jar called *tempayan* is named after the alcoholic brew tapai, meaning the container to brew tapai. Islamisation means tempayan remains only but a name for these jars. The jars, in various sizes, are used to keep water, rice and other household items instead.

Tempeh: A Javanese dish of cooked soya beans that are fermented and then sliced in pieces. The pieces are often wrapped in leaves.

Tiang seri: The main pillar of a Malay or Javanese heart. It serves as an architectural function as well as a mystical function as the 'heart' of the house.

Were-tiger: A creature that morphed from a human being, taking the form of a tiger. Considered to be the darkest of witchcraft by the Malays, were-tigers come in different types and are used for various objectives. At its most evil, it's used for revenge attacks on humans. Strictly hereditary, the Kerinchi tribe of Sumatra is thought to have the ability to morph into tigers, if they choose to practise this dark art. However, the art isn't exclusive to this Malay tribe. The fictional figure for this tale is inspired by the semi-mythical king of Sunda of the Hindu era, King Siliwangi (born 1401), who allegedly practised this dark art. These are rumours but make for a breath-taking speculation. His grandson, Sunan Gunung Jati (1479–1568), however, was a Muslim and therefore didn't practise this witchcraft. The practice was abandoned by the descendants who followed a monotheistic faith.

ABOUT THE AUTHOR

Salina Christmas wrote her first series of horror fiction after more than two decades in journalism and publishing. She studied English Language and Literature at IIU Malaysia and Digital Anthropology at University College London. The horror series is inspired by her childhood during the time of the Second Malayan Insurgency. She was born in Mentakab, Pahang, Malaysia in 1972, where her father's regiment was based. For the first 15 years, Christmas lived in military posts on the outskirts of jungles. Together with her three siblings, including a twin, they attended some ten schools as the family followed their father's regiments all over the country. Christmas grew up listening to plenty of horror stories – real or imagined – and folklore from relatives, teachers and friends. She lives with her sister, co-founder of their product graphic design studio, in London, United Kingdom.

www.ingramcontent.com/pod-product-compliance
Lightning Source LLC
Chambersburg PA
CBHW032034050726
47590CB00006B/2410